# The Vanishing Princess

## ALSO BY JENNY DISKI

### FICTION

*Nothing Natural*

*Rainforest*

*Like Mother*

*Then Again*

*Happily Ever After*

*Monkey's Uncle*

*The Dream Mistress*

*After These Things*

*Only Human: A Comedy*

*Apology for the Woman Writing*

### NONFICTION

*Skating to Antarctica*

*Don't*

*Stranger on a Train*

*A View from the Bed*

*On Trying to Keep Still*

*The Sixties*

*What I Don't Know About Animals*

*In Gratitude*

THE ART OF
ecco
THE STORY

# The Vanishing Princess

*Stories*

Jenny Diski

*Foreword by Heidi Julavits*

Some of these stories previously appeared in the following publications: "The Vanishing Princess" in *New Statesman*; "Sex and Drugs and Rock 'n' Roll: Part II" in *New Statesman* and *New Woman*; "On the Existence of Mount Rushmore and Other Improbabilities" in *London Review of Books*; "Bath Time" in *Sacred Space* (Serpent's Tail, ed. Marsha Rowe).



HarperCollins books may be purchased for educational, business, or sales promotional use. For information please e-mail the Special Markets Department at SPsales@harpercollins.com.

Originally published in Great Britain in 1995 by Weidenfeld & Nicolson.

First paperback edition published in Great Britain in 1996 by Phoenix, a division of Orion Books Ltd.

FIRST ECCO PAPERBACK EDITION PUBLISHED 2017.

*Designed by Michelle Crowe*

Library of Congress Cataloging-in-Publication Data has been applied for.

ISBN 978-0-06-268571-1

17 18 19 20 21 LSC 10 9 8 7 6 5 4 3 2 1

*For Alice, Anna, Emma, Indra and Nell*
*for being such excellent, elegant and witty visitors.*

*And for Chloe, of course.*

# CONTENTS

# Foreword

*Heidi Julavits*

I've been contemplating the phrase *ahead of their time*. What is meant when people are deemed to exist on a temporal plane the rest of us have yet to reach? It sounds like a fantastic compliment, yet the circumstance under which people hear it, in reference to themselves, is not always so positive. People are often told they are ahead of their time as a means of ego consolation following the world's neglect of their work. If they are luckily ahead of their time, the neglect is benign. If they are less lucky, it is not.

Ignaz Semmelweiss, a Hungarian doctor in the late 1800s, tried to convince coworkers that they should wash their hands between dissecting corpses and delivering babies. His controversial "theory of contagion" won him much hostile disparagement and dishonor, after which he suffered a crippling bout of madness (possibly caused by syphilis) and perished in an asylum over twenty years before his theory was, by his doubting colleagues, embraced. So, like Semmelweiss, people can be deemed ahead of their time from a place in the future when the rest of us have finally caught up to the forward-thinking brilliance of the past, by which point the underappreciated (or maligned) innovator who'd out-thunk us by decades is usually dead.

Which is to say: it's best to be told that you're "ahead of your time" when you are no longer alive to hear it.

Jenny Diski, who died of cancer in 2016, just after the publication of her final book, *In Gratitude* (which was, in part, about dying), was ahead of her time. Also, to clarify, while Diski frequented mental wards and suffered numerous suicide attempts in her youth, she wasn't professionally discredited during her lifetime, at least no more so than any writer whose work some people loved and others loved less. Nor would it be accurate to call her neglected; in her native UK, Diski was a prolific novelist, nonfiction writer, and regular contributor to the *London Review of Books*, where *In Gratitude* was first published as a series of essays. Still, I do not think she's received her full due. The literary ledger needs balancing; we owe her a debt.

Twenty-four years ago, in 1993, when Diski published *Skating to Antarctica*, a hybrid work that fused confessional memoir, travelogue, and criticism, she expanded then-current notions about what nonfiction, as an art form, could do and could be. Hybrid nonfiction has, over the decades since, benefitted from the best theory of contagion, mutated and passed along by writers like Geoff Dyer, Hilton Als, Rebecca Solnit, Eula Biss, Maggie Nelson, Wayne Koestenbaum, among others. Still, I find myself embarrassed when I think I know the germination of a literary form and then realize just how wrong I am about history, and how unoriginal we all are, writers and readers, even those of us who might hope to consider ourselves practitioners and fans of a brand-new form.

Diski was, as I've chosen to believe based on her books and essays, under no originality delusions. As Diski writes in her collection's title story—the complete title of which is, "The Vanishing Princess or The Origin of Cubism"—"It was to be many centuries before the form would be invented and by then no one had any notion that it had ever been done before." Diski—again, I choose to believe—was far too shrewd to assert herself as original (in print, at least, though I hope she suffered the momentary hubris and thought it to herself); surely she knew there were writers even more deeply buried in time by foresight than she. Still, it bothers me personally that I came to Diski so late in my reading life, because she was writing the books that I only recently realized I couldn't wait to read, only I didn't have to wait at all, because for decades they'd already existed.

Obviously, thus, I am not a "longtime Diski fan," but a new one. I am playing catch-up on all that I need not have missed. *Strangers on a Train* (2002) juxtaposes memoir and a travelogue of two American cross-country Amtrak journeys. *What I Don't Know About Animals* (2010) is classic Diski in that it unearths the endless questions we might ask, if we were more actively curious, about beings that confront us daily.

Diski wrote, in total, five books of nonfiction and ten—ten!—novels.

I have read none of these novels. My Diski gateway was her nonfiction, and when it came to her fiction, I began with her short stories. The stories collected in *The Vanishing Princess* reveal a writer avidly experimenting with voice and structure and execution. I want to say her stories are "brave" but that sounds blurby and false; maybe it's more useful to describe *The Vanishing Princess* as an artist's sketchbook, a space where play and adventurousness are privileged over snoozy competence and sheen, a preference that seems in keeping with the authentically renegade life Diski, as a person, led.

Diski, born in London, started hard. Sexually abused by her parents, she entered the foster care system and, after meeting Doris Lessing's son in school, was invited to live in the Lessing household. Under Lessing's care she received, in addition to food and a roof and her first years of comparative stability, an apprenticeship in the art of the mold-breaking female writer. Her relationship with Lessing was both formative and prickly, though perhaps this was more the order of the day with Lessing rather than a mark of the uniquely charged chemistry between the two.

And yet, nothing of feminist note feels more renegade—more brave—than Diski's ability, in her final book, *On Gratitude*, to confess to both the debt she owes Lessing and the emotional perplexity that, once she became a mother herself, she felt toward Lessing's life choices. (Lessing left two small children in her native South Africa to move to London and become a writer.) Diski never judges Lessing, and perhaps this quality is what most identifies Diski as a writer: her capacity to accept people and fictional characters and even animals whose lives make no emotional sense to her, but whose existence is no less valuable and compelling and worthy of a good grapple. "I knew the difference as difference," she writes in *What I Don't Know About Animals*, "but difference wasn't a barrier."

The same pragmatic open-mindedness is on display in *The Vanishing Princess*. Originally published in England in 1995, *The Vanishing Princess* collects stories that rove across the aesthetic map. The title story reads like a cheekier, more bitingly urbane take on one of Angela Carter's stories from *The Bloody Chamber*, as does the story "Shit and Gold," a retelling of Rumpelstiltskin in which the miller's daughter critiques, with wry bemusement, the multiply trapped situation in which she finds herself: "Now, it has probably crossed your mind that it's a damn strange thing for a girl to become a wife purely on a the grounds of being able to spin straw into gold. She could become your banker, yes, but why a wife? . . . That's how it goes in this corner of the narrative world: the prize for doing the impossible is to become the wife of a king."

"Leaper" starts on a frank, smart-alecky Grace Paley note before stealthily shifting into oblique emotional territory. (I'd say more about this story but I don't want to ruin anything.) "Bath Time" tracks a woman's lifelong dream to have a perfect bath, and balances the absurd with the penny-pinching real, in a way that might recall the beguiling absurd-real balance in Lessing's *The Fifth Child*. "Housewife," in its cueing of the bawdy, mainstream smut of the 1970s—Judith Krantz's *Scruples*, for example—follows a woman who discovers her sexual self beyond the strictures of the expected female existence, frequently enjoys a slippery vulva state, and experiences many extra-marital orgasms while realizing, with equal shock, that she is "without the faintest remnants of a conscience."

Then there are the more typically realist stories that explore contemporary womanhood from less of a slant. These stories start with lines that appear well behaved such as "It was Lillian's habit to take a walk every lunchtime" and "The thought came to Ellen in the middle of the night." But such opening sentences are not staid pacesetters; instead, they are launchpads. Both Lillian and Ellen athletically muse as a means to analyze, unpack, and cover miles of intellectual and emotional ground between typically disparate landmarks. Lillian starts thinking about ducks and ends up deconstructing her romantic relationship with a man named Charlie, whom she fears is a cheat. Ellen muses about the existence of Mount Rushmore and soon ascends far bigger questions of empathy and uncertainty.

What binds these stories, thus, is their feministly interrogative nature. Most forward-thinkingly feminist is Diski's rattling of words and categories typically used to pathologize actively intelligent women—words and categories like "insane" and "neurotic." Lillian thinks, "It was insane—well, neurotic—to give time and energy to suspicions that made no sense in the light of what was actually happening." Lillian's maybe-cheating-mate Charlie is "remarkably patient with what he called 'LM,' which stood for Lillian's madness.'" (Basically, he's patient with her for being actively engaged in the mysteries of her life, him being chief among them.) Diski calls attention to the ways in which women are taught to doubt their cognitive journeying through quotidian space, while also authentically investigating how personally restricting, in the end, such involuted mental spiralings might be. Diski's strength is her ability to critique her own critique, but from a position of self-awareness: "One problem," Diski archly writes, "was that Lillian was not mystified about why she was like she was."

For me, however, what most distinguishes Diski as a thinker and writer is that she is kind. In all the ways a writer might be considered brave, it is her abundant kindness that marks her as one of the bravest writers I've read, because kindness is not frequently privileged among thinkers for whom superficial sharpness is the easier way to appear incisive and insightful. Kindness in women thinkers is an even riskier gambit; the products of their intellects risk appearing (to idiots) accommodating or soft, and as a result treated with less seriousness. The Diski I've thus far read doesn't get hung up in this mess. She does not equate critical gravity with dismissiveness or hardline bloviating. She does not perform knee-jerk disembowelings as a means to plant the sword of her own intellectual identity on a carcass. She is not intimidated by or made to feel insecure by difference, and so does not respond to otherness with ruthlessness and obstinance. In her stories, her female protagonists respond with engagement, and via that engagement, they often come to understand that they too are a bit wanting; they see themselves differently through investigating the difference of others. Ellen, for example, confused by an inane younger student named Tracy, forces herself to inhabit Tracy's mind. "That it had never crossed her mind that Tracy (and others, certainly) did not know where the eighteenth century was in relation to the present day, seemed to Ellen a level of ignorance close to Tracy's."

So I am sad that Jenny Diski is no longer around to direct us toward the temporal zones we are not yet ready to inhabit; more than ever, the present day feels like one in which we need a person ahead of her time, at least when it comes to the critical challenge of engaging, with open-hearted ferocity, things and people that make no immediate sense to us. Read Diski for the pleasures of Diski, but also read Diski to learn what we may think, in the future, about how, were we possessed by foresight, we might have better performed our humanity in the now.

# The Vanishing Princess

# The Vanishing Princess
# or
# The Origin of Cubism

There was once a princess who lived in a tower. It is hard to say precisely if she was imprisoned there. Certainly she had always been there, and she had never left the circular room at the top of the long winding staircase. But since she had never tried to leave it, it wouldn't be quite accurate to say that she was imprisoned.

The room had a door, and the door had a keyhole, and there was, on the side of the door that she had never seen, a key that hung from a hook in the lintel. She had been put into the room at birth and a series of people, who called themselves relatives, had come and gone, visiting the turret room, opening and shutting the door from time to time. They maintained the lock on the door very carefully, making sure it was always well oiled, so that the princess never heard the key turn in the lock, if indeed it did, and therefore never considered the possibility that she was their prisoner. Since no one ever spoke to her about the world outside the door she came to assume that it was nothing to do with her. She lacked, perhaps, curiosity; but then no one had ever suggested to her that curiosity was a quality to be cultivated. Anyway, she never attempted to open the door from her side, and so never found out if she was a prisoner or not.

But after a while the relatives stopped visiting, and there was a long period when no one came to the room at all. The princess had little sense of time and barely noticed their absence. She spent her days lying on her bed in the circular room, reading the books that filled the shelves that covered the walls from floor to ceiling. Apart from the bed and the books there was a narrow window in the room. Sometimes, when she was replacing a book she had read, or choosing the next, she passed the window. As a child she had seen green fields and woods far off in the distance, and recognised them from the stories she had read. But since her visitors had stopped coming, the land around the tower had grown rampant and it was many years since she had seen anything but vines and creepers covered with briars and merciless thorns. It looked, at the very least, unattractive.

One day, many years after the princess had been abandoned in the tower, a soldier passed nearby. He was a mercenary returning from the last of many campaigns, world-weary and bored with the sameness of everything. He noticed the tangled growth in the distance and wondered at it, that wild forest in the middle of rolling fields. Pleased to find himself curious about anything after so long a period of lassitude, he decided to investigate, and, cutting through the hedges—unworried, soldier that he was, by the merciless thorns—he discovered the tower, and the staircase, and the door to the room where the princess lay on her bed reading books.

The princess looked up from her volume as he came through the door, and waited in silence to find out what he wanted. She felt no great excitement at his arrival, for it didn't seem to her that she was lacking anything in her life. She had what she had always had, and wanted, so far as she knew, nothing.

The soldier questioned the princess about her life in the tower and she told him what little there was to tell: about the relatives who had visited but stopped, about her books, about the view from the window.

"But what about food?" the soldier asked. "When they stopped coming, what did you do for food?"

"Food?" said the princess.

Which was how the soldier discovered that by some means or other, the princess, never having had food, had never learned to need it. This was of particular interest to the soldier, because although he had done everything and seen everything and been everywhere, and was tired of it all, there remained one thing that still gave him special pleasure: the sight of a woman eating excited him as nothing else now could. And though the princess was neither beautiful nor not beautiful, she did have an exceptionally well-formed mouth.

"I'll be back," he said, closing the door behind him.

And as he found an oil-can above the lintel and oiled the lock, the princess couldn't tell whether the key had been turned or not.

The soldier returned, although the princess, having no way of gauging the passing of time, had no idea how long it had been since he had first arrived. He opened the door and saw the princess on her bed, reading. She looked up and smiled. The soldier took the book from her hands and laid a small cloth on the bed on which he placed the food he had brought with him. She smiled again, and, without having to be told, began to pick up this morsel and that, first savouring the smell, then pressing it gently against her lips, and finally tasting. It pleased her, and it pleased him to watch her eat.

Now, at intervals, the soldier came to her with food. Never too often and never with too much. For the princess, food remained a pleasure but never became a necessity. Whenever he tired of his wanderings he would visit the tower with small delicacies wrapped in a white cloth; and she was always willing to exchange the pleasure of her book for the pleasure of food. This went on for many years. The princess came to expect his visits, although, in her timeless world, it couldn't be said that she actually looked forward to them.

Then, one day, a second soldier passed that way. By now rumours had spread abroad about the strange princess in the tower and the soldier who visited her from time to time with small quantities of delicious food. The second soldier had heard these stories and one day, being battle-fatigued and lacking anything better to do, he set out to see if he couldn't find the princess.

He recognised the thicket covering the tower from a good way off and found without difficulty the small path that the first soldier had worn through the undergrowth. When he entered the room at the top of the tower, there was the princess in her usual pose on the bed. She looked up from her book, expecting to see the first soldier and his small bundle.

"Don't be frightened," the soldier said, although such an emotion had not occurred to her before he said it. "I've been looking for you."

And now she did begin to feel alarmed. She had never thought of herself as known in the outside world, and felt a strange distress at the idea of existing in someone's mind as something to be found. The second soldier was a clever man, and noticed her reaction. Being clever, and knowing about the first soldier and the food, he knew he needed an edge. He looked carefully about the room and thought for a long time.

"I'll be back," he said, as he closed the door behind him and oiled the lock. And the princess didn't doubt it.

When he returned he brought with him two objects: a mirror, and a calendar with all the days of the week, and the months of the year laid out for years to come. He placed the mirror on the wall in front of the princess' bed, and nailed the calendar to the door.

"Look," he said, taking the princess' hand and leading her from the bed to stand in front of the mirror. The second soldier had understood on his first visit that it was not only food the princess had lacked all her life.

Having had no way of seeing herself, she had no precise notion that she existed at all. And having had no way to mark the passage of time, she lacked any sense of expectation. The first soldier could come and go, but she did not wait or hope that he would come soon, or this week, or tomorrow.

She looked at her reflection in the mirror, and at first it distressed her. She hadn't seen anything quite like it before. But the second soldier stood by her and she watched his reflection standing next to hers and telling her, "That is you." It took some time, but very gradually she started to think. "Perhaps it is. Perhaps I am here. Perhaps, when people come into this room, they see me." And she looked sideways, out of the corners of her narrowing eyes, at the princess in the mirror.

"When I come to see you," the second soldier said, "that is what I come to see. You."

"Me," the princess repeated, trying to get used to the idea. It was still very disturbing, and yet, there was something about it that she found pleasant. Strange, but pleasant.

"I will come again next week," the second soldier said, and

led her to the calendar to show her how to mark the days. "On this day, Friday, next week, I will come back to see you." And he looked long and hard into her eyes. For this soldier too had something that gave him particular pleasure. He loved to see in women's eyes a look of expectation, a dawning of new possibilities. And the princess had eyes that enabled this to show to an extraordinary degree. But that was not all; the look of expectation was only a part of his pleasure. To complete it he wanted to see that gleam fade to a subtler tone of disappointment.

He returned on the appointed day and watched as the princess' eyes began to show she had understood the nature of time. When he left he gave her another day, and came then too. But on the third occasion he did not come when he had said, but two days later, and there in her eyes was the completion of his pleasure. When he left saying he would be back on such a date, he saw the hope and anxiety mingle in a way he could never have hoped for.

The first soldier did not make a visit during this time, and the second soldier was careful to check that the princess was alone when he arrived. But he left the calendar and the mirror in the room, and she let them remain where he had put them.

When the first soldier came again he looked at both the objects, but said nothing. He laid the food before the princess and watched her lips as she bit off and chewed small mouthfuls. When she had finished he took up the cloth and walked over to the mirror.

"Stand here," he said, pointing to a spot just in front of it. He looked at her reflection for a moment and then took off a diamond ring he wore and, using the edge of one of its facets, he etched the outline of the princess' reflection on to the glass.

"I'll be back when I can," he said, glancing at the calendar, and left.

When the second soldier returned, the princess was pleased to see him, as he came through the door, looking, as she had come to feel, at her. But immediately his gaze fell on the mirror, and the outline etched upon it. He looked first at the princess and then at the glass.

"Stand here," he said, pointing to a spot in front of the mirror, and when she did, he moved her slightly until her reflection exactly filled the outline. The princess looked at herself, and thought, as she always did when she caught her reflection as she passed by to return or get a book, "Here I am."

The second soldier eased a ring from his finger, and with the edge of a facet of the diamond, drew around the reflection of her eyes. First one, then the other. He stepped back to look at it for a moment, then filled in the lids, the pupils and the irises. At last, a pair of eyes stared out from the outline of a woman on the glass, fixed in an expression of longing and alarm so poignant that the princess gasped. She could no longer see her own eyes when she looked into the mirror.

When the first soldier came back he spent at least as much time looking at the eyes in the glass as he did watching the princess eat. When she had finished, he had her stand in front of the mirror and drew her mouth: the lips full and open, mobile and beautiful. The princess could no longer see her lips when she looked into the glass.

Now, on each visit, the soldiers added to the portrait in the mirror. Each soldier examined the work of the other, and then etched a new piece on to the mirror. The outline became no more than a frame, as each man added a feature according to his mood. An elbow was matched with the bridge of a nose; a wrist with a knee; a buttock curved beside an anklebone; one ear rested on a fingernail. Neither man noticed anything that had gone before the other man's last sketch.

Eventually the first soldier stopped bringing food, and the second soldier no longer bothered with the calendar. There came a time when the princess could no longer see herself at all in the mirror. "I'm not here," she said to herself. "Perhaps I never was." And she disappeared.

No one knows exactly how it happened. It could have been that she opened the door one day, discovered that the soldiers had long since stopped locking it, and walked down the winding staircase and vanished forever in the dense, impenetrable forest that surrounded the tower. Or it may have been that, finding herself no longer there, she simply wasn't any more. At any rate, she vanished and no one ever saw or heard of her again.

The two soldiers hardly noticed her absence. They continued to visit the tower, turn by turn, and left their messages for each other on the mirror. The years passed, and, although they never met, their contentment and affection deepened. Eventually they grew old and died. One day the first soldier arrived and found that nothing had been added to the glass. It was not long after that he stopped coming too.

And the mirror rusted, the silvering began to flake away, leaving only scratches on the glass that were indecipherable. When the tower began to crumble, pieces of stone fell and broke the glass itself until there was nothing left of this earliest of examples of Cubist art except rubble greened over with wild vegetation. It was to be many centuries before the form would be invented and by then no one had any notion that it had ever been done before.

# Leaper

He phoned at completely the wrong time, my lover. "Write me a story. A man and a woman, fucking. Keep it short and dirty."

"Fuck you," I said. "If you want a story, speak to my agent. The going rate is £500 a thousand words. If you want a fuck, speak to me. The going rate is . . . what is the going rate?"

"Do as you're told," he said, just the tiniest bit menacing.

"Fuck you," I said, and put the phone down.

I'd spent the morning struggling with a never-to-be-published story and was sunk in a kind of slime of incapacity. What I lack is confidence. Much good it does to know what's lacking. I've written quite a lot: short stories and articles for magazines, most of them published. Looked at from the outside, the writing's going quite well. I've made a small but significant reputation with a number of editors and it's only a matter of time now, before I attempt The Novel that will, I hope, fulfil the promise I've shown.

If that sounds like an efficient piece of PR, it is, because I know, in that place where you really *know* things, that I can't write at all. That fact, that I have produced decent stuff to murmurs of quiet appreciation, doesn't affect this knowledge I have about myself. Something to do with my childhood, I suppose. Anyway, although things turn out more or less all right in the end, it doesn't change anything, and I face every blank piece of paper in a state of panic. This time, I know for sure, they'll find me out.

Things could be worse. That bone-deep knowledge of my own inability doesn't, as it might, pervade my entire life. Not any more. At least it's contained in the writing department, realising, I suppose, that there is where I've decided I can live. I see this now as part of my internal structure; just as there is a language centre in the brain, so I have a worry centre which fills with anxiety and has to find something to worry about. It used to attach itself to anything available: money, sex, shopping, the daily news, the condition of my flat. For no reason connected with anything that was happening, anxiety would erupt. Suddenly, it would occur to me that there was dry rot under the floorboards, or perhaps, since I didn't know one from the other, it was damp rot; and the gnawing worry would infest the day. No matter what sensible things I told myself, that it probably wasn't true, or, if it was, so what, or I could do something about it, the ache would thrum away, colouring the day with anxiety. The damp/dry rot was *desperate* all of a sudden, festering and rotting the fabric of my flat. I would go about my business efficiently enough, but accompanied always in some small space inside me by my fears. By the following morning, the certainty of rotting floorboards beneath my feet would have faded, but something else would take its place, filling up the worry gap before I had a chance to be relieved. A bank statement would arrive and now the money situation, unchanged from a day or a week before, would be terrifying, and I'd spend every free moment listing and relisting my income and outgoings, coming up each time with the same answer, forgetting almost what the problem was, but knowing there was some solution it was essential to arrive at. Sometimes, it made life very difficult to live.

All the time, even in the midst of the panics, I knew it to be free-floating anxiety, its source a well of terror in me that had nothing to do with my chosen concerns. But this information wasn't much help. And sometimes, exhausted by it all, I wanted someone around who would tell me none of it was real, and take away from me the problems that seemed, now and then, to threaten my sanity. But, in fact, I managed, and things have improved. The anxiety is contained.

Now, as I say, since I decided that writing is the only route I've got through life, the worry has latched on to that, like a cattle tick, and gains sustenance from my fears.

What I've learned about this is to ignore it. Most of the time, I write through a miasma of terror, and something decent comes out the other end. I don't know how. I think of it as The Process and leave it at that. It's like swimming in mud; not pleasant, but you get to the other side if you just keep going.

Usually, I can live with the discomfort. Why should things be easy? But occasionally I get exhausted by it, with having to contain my insecurity and generate enough energy to just bloody well get on with it. And still, sometimes, I wish someone else were here to do it for me.

I imagine the conversation with this paragon who will devote his energy to keeping me at it.

"I can't do this. I can't write," I wail, a formless heap.

"Of course you can." The voice is practical, not comforting, even a bit impatient. "What about all the things you've written? You did them, and they were all right. Now, do it again."

"I can't," I howl angrily. "I don't know how those other things happened. They weren't anything to do with me. *This* is the real thing, and I can't do it."

"Well, you're just going to have to try harder, aren't you?"

That's what I'm after. Not soggy comfort, but a hard line. A brusque assumption that I can and will do it, that I don't have any choice. And that, I suppose, is what I do for myself most of the time. But, as I say, sometimes it's hard to conjure up that other voice, and I wish someone else were here to help. Which is foolish, I know, and I get over and on with it. But it doesn't help one bit when Dan calls to play games in the mud I feel I'm drowning in. It doesn't make me feel—I don't know—valued.

I decided it was a good moment to take some exercise. Sometimes I can disperse the panic by working up a physical sweat. I go to a gym just past the local underground station.

As I approached the station, trying to contain my annoyance at Dan by promising it a monumental expenditure of energy on the work-out bench, I noticed that something was going on. Too many people on the street for a weekday afternoon; the bus queue a long, rush-hour line; and small, static groups outside the station itself, standing around in *that* way, signalling an event. An ambulance waited throbbing in the road, traffic building up as cars skirted carefully and curiously around it, its back doors open, red blankets folded neatly on the beds. The entrance to the station, normally a corridor of warm air, a dark gloomy cave into which travellers disappeared, was closed, heavy iron gates pulled across, and behind them, a handful of uniformed figures milled about. Two middle-aged men sat in pale silence on the stone step in front of the gates, neither of them looking as if this was their normal way of being on the street.

I allowed myself the luxury of imagining an electrical fault, an unattended carrier bag, a heart-attack, even, while I walked through the small crowd and beyond the locked gates toward the gym. Where, no longer needing willed ignorance to get past the spot uninvolved, I gave my brain permission to interpret the signs.

There had been a leaper. Some poor but efficient sod had jumped under a passing train.

It's the drivers who call them "leapers." My ex, who likes to know this kind of technical, inside information, met an underground driver in a pub, who told him. Also, that leapers are a bit of a blessing among the lads, since any driver it happens to is given two days compassionate leave, with pay. It always sounded to me like front-line bravado, the brutality of the stomach-sick medical student, the ho-ho-ho of the intolerable. Anyway, "leaper" had stuck with us as a generic term for this particular kind of no-kidding suicide, and that was the word I thought.

I exercised viciously on the sloping bench, jerking the pulleys with muscles that surprised me, so that the weights clanked noisily when they came to rest, and the sliding bench screeched as it rolled up and down the gradient. But no matter how hard I pushed and pumped at the weights, I couldn't drown out the conversation. Two other women had stopped exercising and were standing at the window that looked out over the station.

"What a terrible thing to do."

*Right, that's the word, "terrible,"* I thought.

"Why do you think it's taking them so long to bring the body out?"

*Jesus Christ, think about it. Think hard.*

"You know, my sister was on a train when someone jumped in front of it. They don't let you out. *And* he wasn't killed, the bloke. Not outright. She had to sit there and listen to these awful screams. He screamed and screamed, apparently. She says she won't ever forget it. Can you imagine?"

*Can't blame him, can you? A voice was probably all the poor bastard had left.*

"Terrible. Terrible. Such a terrible thing to do."

I kept my end of the conversation silent and worked on grimly at the bench.

But the conversation continued.

"I suppose we shouldn't be . . . But killing yourself like that, you'd have to really mean it. I can't imagine what it must be like to feel so . . ."

"No. How could anyone imagine it? The poor driver . . ."

When I'd finished my routine I sat in the sauna for as long as I could stand, trying to sweat it all away. Which wasn't long, saunas being unbearable. A Swedish Protestant plot, I think, a stab at hell-on-earth, a dire warning of the discomforts to come. Unsuccessful, actually, since it makes hell-fire attractive by comparison.

Out in the daylight, dehydrated and aching, I looked to my left, in the direction of my flat, on the far side of the underground. Small groups of people still stood outside the station, some in shock, others merely showing a passing interest, a few professionals looking as if this was all in a day's work, some of them succeeding better than others. The ambulance still throbbed and waited. I turned right, and sat at one of the tables outside the café on the other side of the gym.

Recuperate a bit, I decided. You don't have to walk back through and over that drama until you've had a cup of coffee. Sometimes, I'm good to myself.

The woman sat down at my table a few moments later.

It doesn't seem to make much sense, but there's a difference between tables inside a café, and those on the street. Inside, unless everywhere else is taken, it's very unlikely that anyone will ask to share a table that is already occupied. It's a virtual act of aggression, the mark of men on the make and the mildly mad. But it's different in the open. Even if there are empty tables elsewhere, it's an easy, insignificant act to sit with a complete stranger. It must be that people feel they can escape more easily where there are no walls to contain them. And the bright, daylight street seems to exclude the likelihood of whatever it is we fear. Streets are everybody's. Indoors, in the darker interior of the café, the table becomes defensible space, and the approach of another a threat.

I mean to say that I wasn't made uncomfortable by the woman's approach, nor did her presence impinge until she spoke.

She was tall, well built and sleek, in her elegant middle age, with a face that was all bone structure, and dark, spherical glasses. Smooth, dark hair, cut to a heavy, architectural bob, and the clothes tailored (and not in England) to match her perfectly manicured fingernails. Not English. Diane, I was to learn, but think it with a Mediterranean accent: Dee-ahn.

She sat at the table, facing the station in silence for a little while, and then lit a long, dark cigarette.

"Are you watching or avoiding walking over it?" she asked, releasing smoke as she spoke and moving her head slightly to indicate the underground.

"Both, I suppose."

"It will ruin your day if you watch the stretcher come out."

"It's not much of a day, anyway. And a worse one for him or her down there. Or better."

She shrugged lightly.

"Yes. Or no. Her. I understand it was a woman."

There was a quality of utter detachment about her, as though she looked out on the world and saw, but was untouched by it. Everything—her clothes, make-up, the way she sat poised and posed in her chair—looked deliberate and yet it was all so well done that nothing seemed artificial. I hadn't seen her eyes under the sunglasses, but I knew they would be steady whether they looked at me across the table or at the scene along the road. Now she lifted the glasses away from her face and looked me over, running her eyes up and down my body in a slow sweep. Her cool, emerald appraisal was electrifying; the air filled with the static of possibilities.

"Does it excite you, the death down there?"

I took one of her mysterious cigarettes and leaned forward to catch the light she offered. I'm a believer in balance, a serious work-out requires nicotine as ballast.

"I'm thrilled. It astonishes me. I'm bowled over with admiration." Her brow creased in a question. "At the certainty that's been acted on," I explained. "I like a person who knows what they want and leaves no room for indecision or an accident of salvation."

"But what if it were a whim?" she queried. Her deep eyes were amused beneath their steady gaze. "A momentary thing? Irretrievable once acted on?"

I shook my head briskly.

"That's a thought the living use to comfort themselves. *He didn't really mean it.* So that the next time we stand on a station platform we don't have to choose between getting on the train or throwing ourselves under it. We wouldn't mean it, we tell ourselves, we'd be sorry afterwards. What afterwards? The only thing to be sure of is that we *wouldn't* be sorry afterwards. In any case, what makes a momentary whim less true than the thought we've continued to have for twenty years because we haven't bothered to change it?"

She sat back in her chair, resting the coffee cup lightly on her silk shirt.

"The only thing that's true now is the physical end of a life," she said quietly.

I heard my voice, clipped, angry. "Is anything more important in a life?"

"No," she agreed calmly. "But you are a romantic. You will be angry at being told so, but it's true. The fact is that to kill yourself in such a way is childish and aggressive. And stupid, for the corpse down there cannot reap the benefits. Look at the disruption that has been caused. Trains are held up all along the line, people are made late for appointments. Perhaps some of them are important. The traffic is slowed down and passers-by going about their everyday business are drawn in, they cannot avoid being aware of what has happened beneath their feet. Now they feel foolish and petty to be buying a bunch of flowers and a quarter pound of cheese. So much power, so much effect."

But there was no real anger in her voice. It remained distant and melodic. Even a little pedagogical. She continued.

"It makes people think thoughts they do not have to have. That person was living a few moments ago, they think, I might have passed her on my way to the grocer. Was alive, is dead. Only moments in between. As I am alive now, this moment. What is to become of me? What right has someone ending their own life to impose such thoughts on others who may not choose to have them?"

This conversation pleased me. I liked her matter-of-fact, practical assessment of the anonymous death. There was a hardness in her voice that made me listen. And it was a relief to hear those things said. She echoed the thoughts I hadn't allowed myself to have, describing exactly my resistance to walking back over the scene.

I think about death a lot, in a general sort of way. I have a tendency to see it as heroic, a feat. I know we can't help dying, but it's such a serious and solitary thing. Death seems to me to ennoble the most frivolous and incompetent of lives. And voluntary death awes me with its absolute refusal to tolerate the intolerable. I admire the cold calculation, the rejection of a life of fear and panic in favour of decision.

But as I had walked past the underground station on my way to the gym, what I had actually thought was: "I can't stand this."

I couldn't bear the idea of that person's misery as she walked along the street, moments before me, and the terror she felt standing on the edge of the platform waiting for the incoming train. I hated her for making her pain and her death so evident and imposing it on me. It angered and frightened me that she had advertised her safely anonymous unhappiness, and required me to imagine that appalling death beneath my feet.

The truth was I'd had precisely the same thoughts that underlay the conversation I had contemptuously dismissed between the women standing by the gym window, but wouldn't permit myself to say aloud. I couldn't bring myself to admit the common thoughts, banal, true, automatic, human, inevitable, that were being spoken carefully so that the unease could be dispersed by the sound of the words. I prefer to let those thoughts, pointless as I know they are, roll around in the silence between world-weary shrugs. I want them to stay hanging in the air, recognised by their absence. I am, I must admit, ashamed to be on the side of the living.

The woman sitting opposite me, with her brisk tones and coolly interested eyes, voiced my real thoughts and made them seem acceptable. She spoke knowingly, in the manner of a distant observer, of the uncomfortable effects of death on our doorstep. And always her eyes held me in their gaze, faintly humorous, as if commenting, though not unkindly, on my self-deceit.

I heard myself say, "I'm trying to write something. But I can't. I just can't do it."

And held my breath, horrified to hear the words out there in the world, but certain, now that they were said, that she could give me the right answer. I hadn't thought of that harsh, reassuring voice of my imagination belonging to a woman; it hadn't occurred to me, but it didn't seem to make much difference now that I saw it was.

She stubbed out her cigarette with a sudden urgency, as if she had been waiting for a signal and now, having received it, could get on. Putting her glasses back, she smiled, but so slightly it was hardly there.

"Do you have to be somewhere?"

*With you*, I thought.

"No, not really."

"Then why don't we go back to my flat and have a drink? I live just around the corner. It's too depressing sitting here. Why don't we turn our back on this melodrama? Refuse to allow it any power."

She gathered her black leather bag from the table and stood, inviting me to join her.

"My name is Diane."

We crossed the road at the traffic lights in front of the café and she led me to a street directly opposite the station. If we had turned to look in the other direction we would still have been able to see the entrance to the underground. But neither of us did.

The flat was as well-manicured as her fingernails. She made me a drink.

"So you find death exciting?" she said, handing me a large scotch.

"I suppose so."

"And does going home with a strange woman excite you, too?"

"Yes, that also excites me."

She smiled.

"Death has a way of sharpening our desires. It makes us want to eat good food, or listen to a sublime piece of music. Or make love. To lie in someone's arms and feel warm flesh respond to our touch. Death is very sensual, don't you think? The dead have a secret we can't grasp. The secrecy of sex is as near as the living can ever get to it."

Did I say she was beautiful? Apart from all those other things, she was beautiful. Her face was a carved frame for the long, green eyes that looked and looked. Her body was beginning to show its age, loosened a little, but full, ripe and round. I haven't ever rejected the idea of women as lovers, but the event had never occurred.

She undressed me slowly, looking carefully at my body and then checking back with my face. Whatever she saw in it seemed to give her permission not to hurry. When she had finished her slow examination she took off her own clothes, just as leisurely, giving me as much time for taking her in as she had given herself. Then she took me in her arms with as much passion as Dan would show, but it was different. Not his fast, harsh, funny fuck, but a long, slow pleasuring, a drawing out of desire. It was a lesson in timelessness. By the time she led me to the bed she had woven a veil around us with her intricate caresses that seemed to exclude the light. She made the world contract to a capsule containing only the two of us on the white expanse of her bed. And I knew that was what we were there for: to create that veil that confused time and light.

All the while, the green eyes watched with the same humour and detachment I'd seen at the café. But I didn't mind. It exhilarated me that she was in control, building my excitement with careful touches and stroking, checking my response as she increased or decreased the pressure of her elegant fingers and beautiful mouth. Then she took my hand and guided me towards her pleasure. And all of it was more than sensual delight, it was also a promise that she could respond to my *cri*. That she could give me the energy and certainty I couldn't find for myself. Everything she did corresponded to that person in my head who seemed too weary now to help.

I lay naked in her arms, waiting. There was no urgency. I drifted in and out of sleep, listening to the buzz of traffic in the distance, content with the memory of the tone of her voice and the touch of her hands. I knew nothing about her beyond her name and the style in which she lived. But that, along with her capacity to guide me through desire, was enough information, and I had no real curiosity then about her past. Now that I was sated, it was my solved future that interested me. She would, I knew, encourage me and insist I work, understand my necessity, wrap my insecurities in a blanket of her strength. At that moment I thought I had everything. Found, at last, the solution to the panic that threatened to swamp me. I remember the quality of that moment, even now. It was, I think, the first and only time I really felt that everything was going to be all right.

"So you write?"

Her voice was languid and deep, the scent of sex seeped into her low murmur.

"What do you write?"

I lay pillowed in the angle between her arm and breast, smelling the sharp mix of expensive perfume and satisfied desire.

"Stories, articles," I told her, whispering. "I think soon a novel."

I held my breath at the power of the moment, those seconds before one's life comes right.

"You must show them to me," she said, and stroked my hair gently. "I'm sure they must be very good."

And the moment was gone.

I sat up and looked about the room. The afternoon sun poured in through the long windows, washing the beige tones of the furnishings with a warm pink. But I was cold. I wondered for a second if they had brought the stretcher up.

"You met me two hours ago, you can't possibly know whether I can write or not."

I was as confused by my chilly reply as I suppose she was. She sat up beside me and rubbed the side of her face against my hair.

"Well, then, you must show me, so I can judge. I'd like to see the story you're working on at the moment. The one you're having trouble with. We'll have dinner tonight and you can bring it."

I swung my legs out of the bed and stood up.

"I don't show unfinished work. Unfinished work is nothing."

"Then perhaps something you've completed. Bring that so I can see what you do."

She lay back in bed and I began to dress. Everything, suddenly, had slipped from my grasp and I watched as reality wrenched at my fantasy of reassurance and tore it to shreds.

"I don't want to talk about my work," I heard myself say.

"It's not something anyone else can be involved in. You have to do it alone, or it's not yours."

And this, also, was something I knew bone-deep, but had forgotten in the surprise of death and sex and comfort. There is no alternative to the panic and the fear, because it is the panic and fear—and the isolation—that *are* the writing. The desperation created the necessity that made me write. I fed on it.

I was only ever half a romantic, the rest of me, the part that keeps on going, knows how things are and would not swap the final satisfaction of a finished piece for the easy comfort of that voice in my head. I had forgotten that voices in the real world have bodies and intentions of their own—they have flats and furnishings and they make dinner, and need.

I looked at her lying on the bed. She looked to me tired, terribly weary, worn, but her green eyes shone bright and hard still.

"All right." She watched me tie the laces on my shoes. "Dinner without your work. We must get to know each other better. When you're ready I may be able to help you. I have contacts. I can help in various ways. But tonight, just dinner."

She didn't want to be alone, I realised, although there was nothing of that in the tone of her voice which remained cool and steady. And not just tonight. I wondered, at last, about her life.

"Do you live here alone?"

"Yes. I do now. There was someone living here with me, but she's gone."

Her voice was so vague it was impossible to place this information in time. She could have been talking of decades or moments. I felt as if one of us was no longer in the room.

"I must go," I said, turning to the door. "I've got to get back to work. I don't know about tonight. It depends on how the work goes. Shall I ring you later on?"

She reached for a cigarette. The phone rang as she drew on the flame from her lighter, but she made no attempt to answer it.

"Yes, call me later," she said airily, and lay back on the bed watching the smoke spiral through the light beams. The phone continued to make its mechanical bird call.

"Your phone . . ."

"I'm not going to answer it."

"But it might be imp—"

"I know what it's about."

She got out of bed, slipped on a faded silk kimono and moved away from the phone to stand and look out of the window. There was nothing to see except the houses across the road. The phone went on ringing.

"It sounds important."

She inhaled deeply on her cigarette and turned her head slightly in the direction we had walked. From this angle, the station was out of view.

"They will have found this address on Helen. She must have had a letter or something in her jacket, because she didn't take her bag with her."

She turned and glanced at the chair by the door where a tan shoulder bag lay open.

"I suppose they're calling to find out if a relative lives here. They'll be wanting to inform her next of kin."

She spoke more to herself than me, her cool unchanging voice almost inaudible beneath the insistent squeal of the telephone.

"Are you sure you won't come to dinner this evening?"

She looked at me questioningly, her face an impassive sculpture of angles and planes.

"You lived here with Helen?"

The room for all its elegance was a desert, suddenly, an empty cold place being worn away by time.

"Helen lived here for two years. She left this afternoon. She wasn't a happy girl. I tried to look after her, she needed to be taken care of. But some people just won't be helped."

The telephone stopped ringing as she spoke. We both stared at it for a moment. The silence was shattering.

"I must go," I said. "I'm sorry, but I can't stay."

She smiled.

"We must meet again soon. I would very much like to read your work."

But I was already closing the door behind me.

# My Brother Stanley

I knew my brother Stanley only as an oil painting and some photographs. He hung on the wall of the living room, above the sideboard. I thought of it as Stanley's wall. I can't remember if the other walls had anything hanging on them or not. Oh—that's not true; it's much harder to cheat memory than some would have us think. There was, opposite Stanley, a framed print of that greenish oriental lady in a cheongsam, looking cheap and inviting: the one that hung in many an otherwise art-free home in the fifties. These days, I keep my walls white and blank. Nothing hangs on them, perhaps as an anti-mnemonic of the walls of my childhood.

On the gloomy mahogany sideboard which squatted massively beneath Stanley's portrait was a cut-glass bowl which sometimes had fruit in it. It was the sort of thing people were given as a wedding present, but I thought of it as Stanley's bowl.

It had an air of importance and fruit—spotted bananas, pallid apples, we were not big on fruit in my family—never looked quite right in that bowl. It seemed to me more like a trophy, or a memorial object, only masquerading as a useful container.

The oil painting was just a head-and-shoulders portrait of my brother Stanley, his shoulders fading into a neutral greenish background. Stanley looked down from his wall, disembodied. Somehow, I felt the cut-glass fruit bowl was there to make up for the absent rest of him. I don't suppose it was a good painting; in fact, I'm sure it wasn't: there was too great a striving for documentary realism in it, I think, though I'm not much more of an art critic now than I was then. But that was the point, the realism, that was why it was painted; and, in any case, how could it have been other than dutifully realistic when the painter lacked a sitter, who might fidget and chatter his personality into the picture? No, like the bowl, the painting was an icon, and I suppose it was intended to be. Stanley looked down on us, from his ornate gilt frame, present and absent, and the look in his eyes never changed.

I had a way of looking at the painting in private. By manoeuvring two armchairs in a particular relation to each other across a corner facing Stanley's wall, I created a dark triangular cave to huddle in. The arms of the chairs could be raised and lowered, and if I raised both arms I had complete seclusion, except for a carefully arranged crack between them. I spent hours staring at Stanley from my hideaway. Sometimes I just looked at him, but at other times allowed us to look at each other, imagining we each had an eye to either end of the same telescope. His was the end that made things seem more distant than they were, though sometimes, if I gazed long and hard enough, the perspective changed, and I found myself looking at my brother Stanley from an immense distance, a greater distance than any I had ever seen in any other circumstances. That was how I knew how I looked to him, since he had no choice but to stare long and hard and forever.

It was the look in my brother Stanley's eyes that I remember best, though I searched the rest of his features thoroughly to find angles and aspects that reminded me of me. We were, after all, closely related; his father was my father.

The thing about Stanley's eyes was that they seemed to know what was going to happen to him, and that he would be looking out on a future from which he would be absent. The eyes knew that. They were almond-shaped, just like mine—that much we had in common—but mine were very dark, almost black, so that people often said I seemed to have no pupils, or nothing but pupils, depending on how you looked at it. Stanley's eyes were an astonishing cerulean blue, which must have belonged to his mother, or someone long gone in my father's family, because our father's were like mine—black.

Stanley's eyes may have been a vivid blue, but they were not clear—they seemed misted with foreknowledge, occluded with sadness that was matched by two lines on either side of his young, full lips (again, like mine) which seemed to turn the corners of his mouth down slightly. It might have been that Stanley's grave look was what we had in common, some gene that made us seem, in repose, unhappy. People have always told me to cheer up, even when I feel perfectly fine. There's something about my features. "Do you have to look so miserable?" my mother would say when I sat lost and quite contented in a daydream. Or, "Cheer up, love, it may never happen," was the version out in the streets from builders or bus conductors. So I could simply have taken Stanley's gravity for proof of our relationship along with his almond-shaped eyes.

But knowing what I knew of how Stanley's life was to be,

it was impossible not to read loss into his eyes. Even so, I could have concluded that Stanley's expression was the result of the knowledge the portraitist had of his subject. Such a look might have been imposed on those young, blue eyes by an adult's hindsight. But I knew better, because in the right-hand cupboard of the looming sideboard was the very photograph the painter had used as his model. And however limited his artistic talents, the portrait painter knew how to make a good likeness.

In the left-hand cupboard of the sideboard were glasses, bottles of sherry and advocaat which only came out at Christmas. In the middle were cutlery and napkin drawers—all the clutter of respectable dining—waiting (*still* waiting in my unsociable family) for their time to come. In the right-hand cupboard were two—to me—gigantic books. I have one of them still.

Now, I realise, they were not gigantic, just the size of photograph albums. Each book was covered in grainy Moroccan leather and came from Aspreys, which, as my father told me, meant they were very expensive and very special. I knew how special they were just from the smell and the weight of them. I couldn't carry both at the same time to my hideaway (equipped with a torch) but had to make two trips. They were identical except for their colour. One book was a strong air-force blue, the other a rich maroon, with matching stitching. The edges of the pages were gilded a dark gold, like the frame around Stanley's portrait. The blue album was Stanley's, the maroon mine; one for each of us.

Only twenty-four of the thirty-nine pages (not counting the marbled first and last page) in Stanley's book had been used. The photograph that the painting was based on was alone on the twenty-third page. On the twenty-fourth page there were no photos, but there was a daffodil, flattened and dried, like tissue paper that had had its colour bleached by the sun—pale golden-yellow flower, straw stem and dull, dark green leaf—fearfully delicate. After that, the pages were blank.

It was a studio photograph, posed and with a mottled white backdrop, taken in the early 1940s. The painting was an exact replica, except that the photo showed Stanley to the waist, and the painting, as I said, stopped at his shoulders. He was sitting on a stool, probably, as he is rather hunched and round-shouldered the way that children naturally sit when there is no supporting back to their chair. He was wearing a short-sleeved white shirt with a striped tie knotted a little askew at the collar, and over it, a sleeveless ribbed woollen jumper, wrinkled around the waist because of his posture. He hadn't been specially tidied up for the picture, though his side-parted, thick, light brown or dark blond hair looks as if it might have had a comb run hastily through it.

But it was the face that engaged my interest, and particularly the quality of his gaze towards the lens. The painter captured it exactly, but the photograph proved, as I checked from one to the other, that Stanley's look was not a piece of retrospective sentimentality on the part of the artist. It was there in the living, breathing ten-year-old boy on the day he went to the photographer's studio. Stanley's stare is direct and unsmiling.

We never knew each other. Stanley was killed two years before I was born. He wasn't even really my brother, but only my half-brother from our father's previous marriage to a woman whose name I never knew. In the album there are some pictures of her with Stanley. She is elegant and beautiful in that way which women aren't any more, broadfaced, the bone structure not angular, but softly rounded, and she wears delightfully frivolous hats over complex hairdos. She's smiling in all the pictures, gently, lovingly, but it's hard to tell if that was her nature or simply an expression for the camera. There is one photo of her and my brother which is signed, but it's no help so far as her name goes. It says: *To Darling Daddy from Mummy and Stanley, Sept. 9th, 1940.* Of course, there are photos of Stanley and our father. On the beach, walking together along a promenade, in a suburban garden I've never seen, having tea with some old people who must be my paternal grandparents. In these photos also my father is smiling. But again, that's what people do when a camera is pointed at them, and though I do remember his smile, I also remember when he was not smiling.

I was an only child and Stanley was my ghost brother, my friend, familiar, a "guarding angel" (as I thought they were called). It was to Stanley that I would tell all my troubles, wishes and hopes. I seemed always to have known about him. My father told me about him. How he'd sent Stanley and his mother to America to get away from the bombs and yet, having crossed the most dangerous strip of water twice in safety, Stanley had come back only to be knocked down by a bus outside the house. My father said that for some time he was distraught and wandered around London searching for the bus driver (though it wasn't his fault) to kill him. My mother suggested she had come along soon after the accident and helped to heal my father's hurt. The marriage with Stanley's mother had long been as good as over. But once, when my parents' marriage was as good as over too, my mother said, "Now I'll tell you the truth. Stanley was killed because he ran out of the house to get away from their screaming and fighting." I thought I was lucky to live on the third floor of a block of flats—when I ran out of the flat to get away from the rows, there was only a corridor outside.

I dream about those flats, even now, and in reality I pass them probably twice a week or so. In the dream I can only get as far as the lobby, and this is true in reality, too. I walked around there recently, and though the exterior is exactly the same—white stone steps up to glass entrance doors—there is now an entry-phone system which prevents you from going any further without a reason. I don't have a reason, except that I used to live there thirty-five years ago and would dearly love to have a wander round the corridors where I played. There's no real need for it. Just the fact that where my childhood took place is still there, rock-solid but impenetrable. Some people want to climb mountains; I'd like to walk around the corridors.

It was also where Stanley and I were last together. His album and mine parted company in those flats, after eleven years of sitting on top of each other in the sideboard. My father left and took one of the books with him. When my mother and I left the flats some months later, we had no room, in the small bedsitter we moved into, for any more than the essentials. She asked the man who stoked the boilers to take care of some things for her. Among them was the remaining photograph album. It seems odd now that there was not room enough for a photo album even, but things were very fraught and my mother could manage only what she could manage. She told the stoker—Bill, I think he was called—that she would collect the things when we were properly sorted out.

Of course, things never did get *properly* sorted out, and bigger problems arose which made retrieving a photo album irrelevant. Perhaps she just forgot. I didn't, but it wasn't wise to make demands on my mother at that time.

Several years later I was working in an office near to the old block of flats. One lunchtime I phoned the porter's lodge and asked to speak to Bill the stoker. A porter told me he'd left. I explained who I was and that my mother had left some things with Bill. The porter remembered us—we had been rather memorably evicted from the flats—but said that he thought Bill had burned the things when no one came for them. Anyway, he didn't have any idea where Bill was or how to get hold of him.

I didn't press him. I almost hadn't believed that Bill the stoker existed, suspecting he might be no more than a fantasy belonging to a story I'd once heard. But Bill was real enough, and even the porter remembered that we'd left some things with him. As to what happened to them, perhaps it was best to leave that question lie.

In the end, I did get one of the books back. My father died in 1966, and the woman he had been living with gave me the air-force-blue album he had taken with him when he left my mother and me. Back at his house, after the funeral, she handed me Stanley's book. The painting was on her wall. I said I wanted it, but she told me she was keeping it for herself because it had meant so much to my father. We'd never liked each other; I think she felt I was being greedy, asking for both the album and the picture.

I settled for the album, which I still have and look through from time to time. I love Stanley's mother's hats more with each passing decade. And the look in Stanley's eyes reiterates his demand to be remembered. Which, of course, I do. I remember him very well, indeed.

# Bath Time

Eventually, everything had fined down to a single dream. It was this: a bath. But no ordinary bath. It was the perfect bath Meg wanted, the one she had been waiting for, building up to by degrees, as it seemed to her now.

It was perfectly simple, really. She wanted to spend a whole day in the bath. To go to sleep the night before knowing that the next day was her bath day, and wake in the morning and remember that her waking hours were to be exclusively devoted to it.

Easy, some might think, but not so easy, actually. It required the right bathroom, and a hot-water system that could keep the bath at the right temperature for as long as necessary. It meant a day when there were no interruptions: no phone calls, no doorbells ringing, no appointments, guaranteed solitude. Not impossible conditions, either singly or combined. There were probably thousands of people—more, hundreds of thousands maybe—who had, or could create, the right circumstances. But, for one reason or another, Meg had never managed to achieve a combination of all the circumstances needed for the day-long bath. The day-long bath was a notion that had come to her more than eighteen years ago, but which she had never been able to put into action because unless everything was right, there was no point. And *everything* had never been right at the same time.

The size of the bathroom was not a factor. Meg was perfectly happy in small rooms; unused space tended to make her anxious. The bathroom she had had as a child was perfectly adequate, she remembered, though no larger, in the tiny two-roomed flat, than it had to be to contain the bath, washbasin and toilet. It was clean, neat, and although she couldn't actually visualise the walls, she supposed that they must have been a bathroom sort of colour, pale pink or *eau de nil*. Not to her present taste, but she didn't think she'd have minded as a child. The actual suite, as they say, she was certain was white. Baths and toilets didn't come in any other colour then, unless you were a starlet or a duchess. Still, satisfactory as it was, as a physical environment, when she remembered that first bathroom, it was with fear. She always saw herself sprinting from it, dragging her knickers up from around her knees as she ran, while the waterfall rush of the cistern filling up threatened to engulf her. It was always essential to get out as fast as possible after she'd pulled the chain—yes, it was a proper chain, hanging from the raised cistern. She always left the door open, of course, to facilitate her escape, once the time had come when her parents had insisted that the toilet had to be flushed.

Water had scared her, then. She used to wake at night screaming, and when her mother arrived would tell her that she was afraid of drowning in a flood. It did no good for her mother to point out that it wasn't raining, there was no flood, and that, even if there had been, Meg was not at risk in her bedroom on the fifth floor of a block of flats in the middle of London. The flushing of the toilet seemed to Meg a premonition of rising waters breaking down the brick walls, seeping, then surging, through cracks in the window frames, and overwhelming her. She was aware from a very young age, for no reason she could now fathom, of the lethal power of massed, fast-moving water.

The only thing she remembered distinctly about the first bathroom was that her mother always poured disinfectant into the bath when she ran it for her daughter. She could see the bottle of Dettol up-ended in her mother's hand and the brownish orange liquid hitting the clear bathwater in a thin stream, instantly clouding it. It seemed like a magician's trick, or later, when she heard the story at school, the miracle of Christ changing water to wine. But she wondered also what germs she carried that her mother battled against. Dirt was dangerous, of course, there was no doubt about that. Her mother cleaned the flat and washed clothes and herself with a vigour that plainly was keeping something terrible at bay. Illness, the plague, perhaps? But that wasn't really it—her mother had no understanding of the virus theory of disease, colds came from wet feet, flu a willed perversity on the part of her daughter to make cleaning activities next to impossible. Mrs. Tucker was keeping away dirt, which she called germs, because it was *bad* and threatened the fabric of *niceness* which it seemed to be her job to maintain against all the odds. She put Dettol in her own bath, as well as her daughter's, and complained each morning, her face heavy with disgust, about Meg's father's casual attitude to cleanliness.

"He never washes above his elbows," she would say, hissing almost, at the horror of it, as she scrubbed vigorously between her legs at the washbasin. "I'd rub myself away if I could, keeping clean. He only has a bath at the weekend because I nag him. Filthy pig."

Mrs. Tucker had had an impoverished childhood, deprived of everything, as she told Meg, including the luxury of a bath and hot running water. The germs, Meg came to understand, were mainly to be found in that area that her mother paid so much attention to in the morning. Her mother stood naked at the basin, her legs apart, and washed down there as if her life depended on it, while Meg sat in a foot and a half of opaque, pungent water, watching. She concluded it was from that place between her legs that the dirt originated and where the Dettol was supposed to do its germ-assassinating work. Meg wanted bubble baths and creamy soap like she'd seen on the television, but always it was milky, sharp-smelling water and coal tar soap, and every nook and cranny to be washed so that when she called her mother to tell her she'd finished she could answer each element of the litany—"Have you washed your . . ." (the list included all the cracks and crevices that might be passed over by a haphazard washer)—with a truthful "Yes."

Leaving home had been no hardship, she'd had enough of her mother's scrubbing of things and herself, enough of her father's tight-faced loathing of everything his wife and his miserably small, clean home represented. She went with a light heart to teacher training college and the flat she would share with four other students. Then, the world was full of promise.

The bathroom, however, was a disappointment. Well, hardly a disappointment, only to be expected, really. The flat was soon covered with cheap and cheerful things to negate the unaltered fifties drab. She and her flatmates flung colourful bedspreads over dull moquette, put up posters of the Beatles and other dawning heroes of the hour and lashed out on a set of stripy mugs to drink their instant coffee out of. There wasn't much that could be done about the bathroom. That one *was eau de nil* (though pock-marked by patches where age and damp had flaked off the paint), and by now Meg minded. The lino was icy and cracked, wind whistled in from a broken corner of the window, and there was no kind of heating. But there was, as her mother would have pointed out, a bath and hot running water. At least, it was sometimes hot, and it did run, though so slowly you could write the best part of an essay while waiting for it to fill even a third full. It was a huge, cast-iron bath, with claw legs, of the kind that later would become much sought after, but this one was chipped and caused the already lukewarm water to chill almost as soon as it finished falling from the chrome swan's neck tap. The water heater made such terrible, threatening noises, clanking and burbling, that Meg and her friends would turn it on at arm's length as the pilot light whooshed the flames into action, and then run for their lives back upstairs to their room, just in case, this time, it really did explode.

But none of this was unusual. It was what students' digs were like, what most people's homes were like. Things changed very slowly. And for Meg and her friends it was part of the fun of being independent at last. Waking up in the morning, dashing down to the bathroom, freezing feet, freezing water, a quick memorial swish with the toothbrush, it was all as they expected, and fun with it. Meg hadn't developed the notion of the day-long bath at that point in her life, but she could, and did, make some changes. For one thing, she bathed only once a week, like everyone else (and like her filthy pig of a father) because no one could afford to feed the meter for more baths than that on a small student grant. But she did set aside enough money to buy herself a bar of Imperial Leather soap and, once a week, one squashy plastic sachet of vividly-coloured bubble bath. Nothing fancy, but she was prepared to risk her life with the immersion heater for long enough to cut the corner of the sachet and watch as the squeezed liquid turned the water blue, or green or pink, and, even in the slow stream of the immersion-heated water, began to form bubbles quite as luxurious-looking as in the advertisements.

She lay, or tried to lie (the bath being too big and slippery), for as long as the bubbles lasted—which wasn't long—in spite of the rapidly chilling water. It was a hint, at least, of baths that might be to come, just as a passionate grope, curtailed by a flatmate's early arrival home, was an embryonic taster of long, languorous hours of love, once the circumstances made it possible. Whatever discomfort Meg and her friends put up with, it was with the unspoken assumption that their lives would develop, financially and socially, to the point where things would be just right and comfortable with it. But for now, at least there were no more Dettol baths.

Meg couldn't, however, remember that bath with much affection. It was the place where, in her last year at college, the mess that resulted from the combined effect of the bath (made extra hot with kettles of boiling water), the bottle of gin, and the dubious—but, as it turned out, effective—pills, came away from her. She hadn't been very pregnant, no more than a particularly heavy period left her and turned the water pink and mucky, but, relieved though she was, her head reeled at the sight of what was supposed to become a baby swirling away, in a livid, turbulent whirlpool, down the plughole. She wished then, quietly to herself as her friends helped her out and dried her off, that she had a bottle of Dettol.

Over the next few years of being a student and then a probation teacher, there were several more, only gradually improving, bathrooms of a similar kind. The only really notable one, the one out of the lot of them which remained in her mind's eye, was as dingy and unwelcoming as all the rest, although it was enhanced by having one wall covered with mirror-like paper and a couple of posters of Jimi Hendrix that had curled at the edges from the damp. But it was where Meg learned not to hate washing her hair. Then, her hair was long, flowing—as it was supposed to do, like heavy, rippling liquid—down her shoulders to the soft, equally flowing lines of tie-dyed, Indian cotton, full-sleeved blouses and long skirts. It was an endless business, washing and drying her hair. Sometimes it would take Meg a fortnight to build up the necessity to the point where it was unavoidable. The bath did have a rubber hose attachment that could be pushed on to the tap, but crouching bare-topped in the cold bathroom was a dismal business, until the day she washed her hair while under the influence of LSD.

Waterfalls poured on her upside-down head, tiny drops of wet light, fragmenting into colours of minute and jewelled brilliance so that her saturated hair twinkled messages like psychedelic stars in a multi-stranded universe. The feel of foaming shampoo squeezing through her fingers was indescribable, unearthly. When she rubbed her hair dry, the colours that had sparkled in the droplets of water jiggled inside her head as if her brain were a kaleidoscope, and the smooth wet strands were a beaded curtain that swished aside and let in shafts of light like a Cubist painting. All in all, a thoroughly excellent experience, and although she never washed her air on acid again, the memory remained.

That was the same bathroom where Doc used to shoot up, and where, as Meg sat on the edge of the bath, watching him perform his ritual, he told her one day, after the H had hit, that he had found an incredible cottage in Sussex they could share with another couple he knew, and what about getting out of London and the hassle of everything? It was near enough for him to get his supplies—the other couple were both addicts—and they could organise enough stuff between them to keep everything sweet. Meg, who did not use heroin, but who often washed out his syringes for him in a curious transformation of domesticity, appropriate to the time, stared at Doc. For a second, she imagined a cottage bathroom, roses on the wall, wooden towel rails, a pretty chintz curtain, a deep-grained oak window ledge with scented things for bath and body. Then, as she visualised it, she saw it littered with used syringes, smears of blood inside the transparent tubes and spots of it congealing on the tips of the needles.

"No, I'm not going," she said.

Doc said nothing, but rolling down his sleeve, walked out of the bathroom, packed his small leather suitcase, took his books from Meg's shelf, leaving curious gaps, and left. She never saw him again.

With the passing of flower-laden peace, Meg's life took a turn towards the more conventionally domestic. Marriage to Peter, who, like Meg herself, had also only been passing through a period of dissolution, provided a new bathroom. An entirely new bathroom. New walls, new floors, new ceilings, new everything. They bought a derelict house, and with the aid of a council grant—a piece of lost history, if ever there was—Meg and Peter carved a bathroom out of a large, unused cellar, just in time for the arrival of the baby.

It was the largest bathroom of Meg's life, square and roomy and designed for living in as much as for cleanliness. Either Meg or Peter would lie in the bath with the new baby beached, like a small, gurgling whale, on their chest, while the other parent sat in a wicker chair chatting about their day—Peter teaching, Meg indulging herself full-time in baby care—or reading snippets of the newspaper aloud. And when Florence was asleep in her cot, there was enough room on the floor of their bathroom for Peter and Meg to make love on a towel, after soaping each other in the cramped but friendly bath.

Since the entire house had to be renovated, the grant—decent though it was—had to stretch as thin as strudel pastry. Living rooms and bedrooms got priority and were finished: white walls, bookshelves, brightly-painted furniture in the baby's room, stripped pine everywhere else. But the kitty was empty just at the time when they were ready to decorate the bathroom. The bath and everything was there, plumbed in and working, the walls were smooth and pink from Peter's remarkably effective plastering skills, but there was no paint on the walls, no covering on the cement floor, and, because it didn't seem important, no door or doorframe in the empty rectangle prepared for them.

No one minded. Certainly not the baby, who had no history of bathrooms, nor Peter or Meg. It was, in fact, the best bathroom Meg had ever had. It was warm, with *two* radiators as she had insisted, it was clean, and the water ran from the taps fast and hot. The lack of a door didn't present a problem. After a few months of nappy changing, cleaning up baby vomit and scrubbing dried pulped food from the kitchen chairs and floor, privacy didn't seem an issue, certainly not worth going into the red for. It was true that when the grannies came to visit they complained, and other people, though wishing to appear laid-back, took to whistling while they had a shit, but Peter and Meg weren't bothered enough to do anything about it.

But it was then that Meg thought about the day-long bath and realised, best bathroom of her life though it was, that here it was not possible. It was very rare for an ordinary bath to be uninterrupted by Peter popping in to chat, or ask what they were having for dinner. Even when Peter was at work, Florence would come crawling and beaming through the unfinished doorway, or worse, remain silent, forcing Meg to get out of the bath every ten minutes to make sure she was still playing quietly with her crayons in her bedroom. Moreover, hot though the water was, there was no chance of keeping it that way for the hours she fantasised, because it took a whole tank to fill the bath, and then it was at least an hour before the water was hot again. Just not the right conditions, though Meg did develop her concept of bathtime. In her mind now, there were two kinds of bath: the working bath, where she soaped and scrubbed, washed her hair, shaved her legs. The business-like bath. The other kind had nothing to do with being clean. It was about lying submerged to the chin in scented, oiled water whose heat seeped through her skin and into the very marrow of her bones. Warmth was the point of this kind of bath, a warmth that didn't seem available anywhere else; not in Peter's arms, not in the baby heat of Florence against her breast. It was a private, solitary stoking of her fires, and one she began to wish she could prolong.

But when Florence was eight, the bathroom plaster had lost its bright pinkness and the cracks (Peter being a good, but not professional plasterer) had become too big not to notice. The lack of a door suddenly became something of a problem, although it took a while for Meg to understand this. Peter had always disappeared into the bathroom on a Sunday with a pile of colour supplements, but now he started to announce his visit.

"I'm going to the loo," he'd say.

Meg was faintly surprised at first, because it didn't need saying, but she gradually realised that what he meant was, "Leave me alone, don't come wandering in and start reading one of the papers on the floor and discuss interesting recipes you've come across." His announcement about visiting the loo was the same as bolting the door, had there been one. Meg shrugged and kept away after being snapped at several times.

"Do you mind!"

But then she noticed that for some weeks—or was it months?—she had been bathing after Peter had gone to bed at night, only getting out once she was sure he was fast asleep. Neither of them could say, "I want a door on the bathroom," because it was obvious that it would be tantamount to saying, "I want a divorce."

The next bathroom *was* painted. It was white and had perfectly acceptable greyish vinyl tiles on the floor. It was the most civilised bathroom of her life. Small, efficiently designed, and when had she ever had a bathroom cabinet to keep—not Dettol—make-up, cotton wool, TCP and burn ointment neat and out of sight? The flat was big enough for just the two of them, Meg and Florence, and was a typical newly-converted, square, paper-thin walled series of boxes, but it looked nice enough. But the day-long bath was still out of reach, not just because she could not solve the problem of keeping the water hot, but because the idea of having the bathroom to herself for an entire day, or even an entire hour, was laughable.

Between the ages of ten and fourteen, Florence made the bathroom her very own, as much her territory as her bedroom. It seemed a necessary part of her development. The mirror, the make-up (Meg's), bath oil, shaving foam, razors, scissors, tweezers, became essential adjuncts to Florence's daily life. Meg would try to point out that the bathroom was shared, and that her make-up was not, but Florence's need for self-definition caused her memory to blank on the subject. Meg got used to using the bathroom in those odd moments when Florence had vacated it, collecting damp towels that had been strewn on the floor, saving lidless pots of creams and open wands of mascara from drying out, before she could run her bath.

During the day she worked, back at teaching, because being a single parent she could not afford the luxury of choosing poverty and daytime access to her bathroom rather than earning a living. And although Florence spent every other weekend with her father, Meg still didn't have the bathroom to herself, because that was the only private time she and Jack had together for unfettered love-making, what with the thinness of the walls and the compactness of the space. She didn't feel she could tell him he couldn't come round on alternate weekends because she wanted the bathroom to herself.

Eventually, however, Jack had receded into amiable friendship, and Florence left home, successfully reared, disappearing into university life and travelling vacations. All the years of gazing at herself in the mirror, trying on alternative faces, different eyebrow shapes and lip outlines had, astonishingly, turned her into an elegant but thoughtful person clearly on her way to becoming a committed and successful lawyer. The day she announced that she was sharing a large house near her college with some friends, Meg put the flat on the market.

She looked at numerous properties, but she could not make the estate agent understand that she meant what she said when she asked to see a flat in need of total redecoration. He assumed a woman of her age would want something nicer, but she explained that she had very special plans and could not afford to dismantle something that was already in place to put in what she wanted. But, the estate agent explained, for the money she had, she could get a decent place with everything in good order even if it wasn't exactly the order she wanted.

"But I've got very special plans," Meg explained again, patiently.

Eventually, with some distaste, the estate agent showed her a flat that was near-derelict in a dingy road of dreary terraced houses.

"I can get you something much better," he kept saying as they creaked up the stairs, Meg taking care not to catch her heels in the holes in the filth-encrusted carpet.

But it was just what she was looking for. The house had been left empty for several years as the owner, hoping to sell to a property company hungry for an investment, found himself stuck in the downward-spiralling house market of the late eighties. Eventually, he put each of the two flats on the market at a price which meant, even though Meg sold her flat at a loss, there was some money left over.

Not much, not enough to repair and renovate the flat into something decent and comfortable to live in, but enough for what she wanted to do.

"I'll take it," she said.

The estate agent shrugged, happy enough to get any kind of sale, the way things were.

Meg was not gifted with practical skills. The amount of money she had to spend on the renovations was small, but it was enough to employ a builder to do what she wanted. She found one in a local paper and showed him the job.

He walked around the flat, digging his heel professionally into soft spots in the bare floorboards, and pressing his palm against ugly stains on the wall, muttering, "Dry rot, here," and "Damp, I'm afraid."

"Don't worry about that," Meg said, steering him past the uninhabitable rooms.

He noticed, in one of them, a made-up mattress on the floorboards, and a metal clothing rail.

"You're living in this place?" he asked. "In this condition? Haven't you got anyone you could stay with until the work's done?"

Meg was ahead of him and had reached her destination.

"Here. This is what I want sorted out."

She handed him the sheaf of papers she was carrying.

"I want it done exactly like this."

The builder looked at the drawings. They weren't professional, but they explained well enough, and in minute detail, what the customer wanted.

"Yeah, okay. This looks fine. And what about the rest of the flat?"

"A boiler. Just a boiler."

"Central heating, you mean?"

"Just a boiler," Meg said again. "There's no need for radiators."

The builder stared at her. "All right, then. Now, the rest of the flat?"

"That's all. The bathroom and the boiler. That's what I want done. That's all I've got the money to do."

"You can't live like this," he said, and concentrated hard on the specification she'd handed him. "You know, you could do this much more cheaply and there'd be enough left to get the basics done on the rest of the flat. You've got to have a kitchen, and the bedroom and living room aren't habitable."

"I want the bathroom done *exactly* as I've explained."

The builder was about to argue and opened his mouth, but then thought better of it. This one was a crazy, he decided, and a job was a job, especially these days. He shrugged.

"You're the boss, mate," he said. "When do you want me to start?"

It had taken six weeks to level the floor, put in a damp-proof course, strip and replaster the walls, find a bath of exactly the required length and build it in, plumb in the other fittings and decorate to the client's requirements. The longest job was the tiling—from floor to ceiling with four-inch glazed white tiles, and six-inch white ceramic tiles on the floor. It wasn't a large space, but the tiler, near desperate towards the end of the job, worked out it had taken four thousand and seventy-three to cover the walls. He started on the floor with the light heart of a Cinderella who had only a few more beans to pick up before she could go to the ball. Then the fittings were put up. These were minimal. One chrome towel-rail, a glass shelf above the washbasin and another running the length of the bath. The small window was reglazed and the frame and ceiling were painted with four coats—no, three would not do, Meg had insisted to the painter—of white eggshell. Then the new boiler was installed—a combination boiler that harked back to the old immersion heaters of Meg's past. It heated water directly from the mains as it was drawn through to the taps, needing no storage tanks. Meg, at last, had a good, constant flow of hot water to top up a cooling bath.

The bathroom was finished just in time for the Christmas holidays. Florence was off to North Africa with a boyfriend and Meg announced to friends on the verge of inviting her to Christmas lunch that she was going away, too. There was very little money left, but she had costed the bathroom with great care, so there was enough for the final essentials. She did not, of course, mend the doorbell that didn't ring when pressed (indeed, with the aid of the builders' tools, she unscrewed the knocker that the builders—her only visitors—used to gain entry). Nor did she use any of her precious funds on installing a telephone.

Meg spent the first days of the holidays buying white towels, a variety of astonishingly expensive French designer foaming bath oils, and a chrome rack to place across the bath that had a place for soap, flannels, *and* a book stand attached with a small chrome tray next to it, just the right size to hold a wine glass.

Then, when everything was in place, she took the time to stand in the doorway—with a door and a lock—and inspect her new bathroom. Behind her, and to each side, the rest of the flat remained as derelict as the day she had bought it, but she didn't notice, or care. She stared into the bright bathroom and her eyes almost ached with its gleaming whiteness. It was, for all the time and money lavished on it, quite spare. There was nothing in it except white tiles, a carefully-folded white towel and the white bath, washbasin and sink. The fittings were silvered chrome and glass. Meg had ditched her make-up—she had thrown away everything from her previous bathrooms. There was a square-edged black bottle of scented bath oil and some discreet pots containing face packs and washing grains on one end of the long glass shelf on the tiled wall above the bath, and a neat pile of books on the other.

New bars of plain white soap waited on the bath tray and the washbasin. There was a white electric toothbrush and a dispenser of toothpaste, from which she had taken off the label, so that it too was plain white on the glass shelf over the basin. Meg surveyed this bathroom that she had made, and found it good.

It was Christmas Eve, and Meg sat in the old chair she had brought from her previous flat, in her empty living room with peeling walls, eating a takeaway from the Chinese place round the corner. Tomorrow would be the loveliest day of her life.

She listened to the boiler humming quietly to itself, in constant readiness to produce however much hot water was required. Nice. Something really special to look forward to. How many people had lived their lives up to the point Meg had reached and could say that they were about to fulfil their great ambition? Only a few, she suspected, among the millions, who would look back at the end and wonder how they had missed their moment. Meg's moment had come. Tomorrow she would have the Christmas Day of her life. You only had to know what it was you really wanted, she told herself, wrapped in her duvet in the freezing, desolate room, with the smile of a cat savouring the prospect of tomorrow's bowl of cream.

# Housewife

*Creature, you've made me crazy. I ache for your dark passageways and serpentine corridors. Those coiled, labyrinthine, unlit spaces, saturated with mysterious liquors unknown to those who avoid the shadows, which are the antechambers to your underworld. A traveller returning from these places (and few do) can never be entirely happy in the sunlight again. Forever after he retains the scent and taste of his unspeakable adventures, which return to distract him in the normal course of his life, so he has to stop whatever worldly activity he's engaged in (marking essays!) and close himself away in a dark room to pay sinister homage to the memory of where he's been and what he's known.*

*It's a curious fact that quite ordinary incidents bring the flavour and perfume of his time in the dark country back to him: the accidental brush of a silk scarf against his skin, washing certain parts of his body (you know which), or merely tightening a watch strap around his wrist, causes the most acutely painful and (as he would describe it) exquisite recollection of the dripping pungent juices in which he was once submerged.*

*Sometimes in the subterranean traveller's dreams, he returns and sleepwalks through the drenched corridors again. The danger and his secret hope is that he will drown and never wake. The dreams are so real and the desire to take in enough of the secretions of the place so great that he covers himself completely and fills every orifice—eyes, mouth, nostrils, ears, anus—with the fluids, which have become more than food and drink for him.*

*Of course, once all the entrances to his body are moistened, the creature which inhabits the dream labyrinth is free to enter them, probing all the secret places, inserting tongue and fingers into its hapless visitor, loving the tastes that emerge from the fusion of its own tainted secretions with his. It spreads the wetness all over the body of its prey, and then squats over it, showing the traveller what it was he came to find—the saturated source of its power—before lowering itself on to him, smothering him under its weight, covering him with the sweet and sour slime he longs for.*

*After that, the traveller is the creature's thing, to do with what it will. And it does everything, leaving him and taking him at whim, a playful creature which loves to toy with its plaything, covering him with its juices and then very slowly licking them off with the tip of its tongue until every part of his body had been covered, and it can start to smear him with its filth again. There's no escape, now, only waiting and repetition. But that's all right because it is all the traveller in the dark land wants.*

*Creature. My witch. My Kentish whore. Do you realise what power you have? You never disappoint me.*

About an hour after she'd seen the children off to school, the postman rang the doorbell with a parcel. It was addressed to her personally: Mrs. Susan Donahoe, 14 Paramount Close,

Sidcup, Kent. She hadn't been expecting anything. Sometimes, she received parcels when she ordered clothes from the Next Directory catalogue, or bought thermal underwear by post for the family, but she hadn't ordered anything recently and, in any case, this parcel was the wrong shape for clothes. It was registered, so she signed for it and thanked the postman with a smile.

She put the rectangular package down on the kitchen table. Its brown wrapping paper was neatly folded into Vs at each end, their apexes just touching and held down with sellotape, the whole parcel being doubly secured with firmly tied and knotted string, which she cut with the kitchen scissors—once she'd found them in the cluttered drawer where the utensils were kept. The size and shape of the parcel was familiar, and when she pulled back the wrapping paper, she wasn't surprised to find a shoebox underneath. It was also crossed with string, and rather battered as if it had been lying at the bottom of someone's cupboard for some time: it wasn't a new pair of shoes she'd ordered and forgotten about. In any case, Susan wasn't one to forget things.

Still baffled, she severed the string and put the lid to one side without noticing a piece of paper, folded and sellotaped to its underside. The interior of the box was lined in several layers of black plastic, cut from a black bin bag, which overlapped at the top, covering what was inside. She lifted them away carefully, and saw a fastened package made from the lower half of another bin bag. Susan untwisted the wire closure tying off the opening, to reach, finally, whatever it was she had been sent.

When she peered inside, she gasped, and instinctively turned around as if to check that no one else was in the room, although she knew she was alone in the house. Then she turned back, and sank sidesaddle on to the pine breakfast bench beside the table, to gaze into the shoebox in front of her. Lying in a pool of its own blood was a whole, raw, pig's liver of a red so deep it was almost black.

The rank smell of blood and offal, released into the air, billowed up, assaulting her nostrils, but she was too stunned to move her face away from the acrid scent. She stared concentratedly at the liver's satiny bulk, noticing the way in which it graduated away towards its boundary to a fine edge, and how the light from the kitchen window made its sloping, slippery contour gleam. It was an extraordinarily substantial object.

Susan kept her eyes on the contents of her parcel, as she pulled the wrapping from under the box, but the label, when she looked at it, was printed and the postmark smudged. Reaching for the lid, she saw the paper taped to it. She dragged her eyes away from the offal to read the message. "Longing for you." There was no signature.

Susan's mouth compressed into a tight line, her teeth biting down hard on the inside of her lips, and the vertical frown lines of a face straining to compose itself appeared between her eyebrows. Then, in spite of her efforts, she lost control; her mouth opened, her eyes closed and Susan let go with a gale of delighted and wicked amusement as the laughter she had been trying to suppress snorted explosively through her nostrils.

*Dearest Witchfinder—Of course, you're never disappointed. How could you be? Since when was a dream disappointed by the dreamer? Don't you know that what you dream is what I dreamt up for you, my dreamed-up lover, to dream? Your pleasure coincides precisely with my pleasure. How could it be otherwise?*

*Realise my power? No, you realised it. You found and recognised me, Witchfinder Very Particular. But now that I know, I'm working on a spell for turning literature lecturers into bats (selected ones, that is, not all of them) so that you can fly through a crack in my belfry late tonight and have your way with me. Alternatively, I'll go bats myself and swoop down on you, and very quietly, so as not to disturb anyone, I'll take your soft, sleeping cock in my hungry bat mouth and gorge myself, chirping at an inhuman pitch, until the dawn. You'll only know I've been there by the strange dreams you'll dream. Misty, murky things, like swamps, with smiles hanging from the trees.*

*I'm your thing, utterly, completely, for more and more, without limits. Sometimes I think I can still smell you on my pillow, even though we change the bedding. I carry on as normal, but I think I am really quite mad. I know I am. Be kind to bats. And leave your window open just a crack.*

When the doorbell rang again, at midday, it was not unexpected. By then, Susan had bathed and washed her hair, taken her make-up out of the bathroom cabinet and applied it carefully, almost meditatively, to her cheeks, eyes and lips. From an M & S carrier bag tucked away at the back of a top shelf reserved for old clothes, destined (when she got around to it) for Oxfam, she extracted an elasticated wisp of a suspender belt, sheer black stockings and a pale silk slip, not destined for Oxfam, and put them on her newly pampered and lotioned naked body. She dressed herself in these undergarments slowly, with pleasure, and a half-smile on her face which once or twice broke into a broader amusement at the memory of her package that morning. When she had finished she opened the wardrobe door with the long mirror on the back of it and stood back to look herself over.

Susan was no stringy-limbed waif, but a sturdy middle-aged woman with what her mother had called "big bones." She stood and examined her solid fleshy self in what she was amused to call her *lingerie*, to distinguish it from her regular M & S *underwear*, and decidedly liked what she saw. Susan Donahoe, who dressed as a rule for the life that was led in Paramount Close—practically in skirts and jumpers for the daily round, tidily in suits for parents' evenings and "do's," comfortably in tracksuits for Sundays at home with the family—stood before herself with satisfied approval as the luscious, sexually shameless slut Mr. Donahoe had never known. Nor had Susan, if it came to that, not until recently.

The soft fleshiness of her upper arms and shoulders, and the ripe, dipping cleavage between her large breasts (maternal, was how she usually thought of them, big suburban boobs) was accentuated and made all the more lush by the fragile straps, slivers of oyster silk, and delicately rolled edge of the slip which barely seemed to contain the flesh it enclosed, and yet smoothed its contours with the fluid satin fabric. After a moment, she lifted the slip above her thighs, whose softly substantial nakedness, like her shoulders and breasts, was emphasised by the vertical line of the suspenders and the encircling tops of her stockings. Flesh and fabric alternated: offering more, offering less, leading the eye up towards the dark, curled mass of hair which concealed and emphasised what lay behind it. She loved the lewdness of it.

She loved how she looked, more than she had liked herself, firmer and somewhat slimmer (she had never been a sylph), in her youth. In those days, she might have admired herself for what others had admired about her: as a good-looking English rose, a blossoming buxom girl dressed for the world to see on her way to the theatre, or some party, on the arm of a pleasant if not exciting young man. Now, two decades and more later, she felt almost dizzy with excitement at the sight of herself, large, loose, her flesh lived in and entirely sexual, totally available. The silk and lace sheathed those parts of her which she most dearly wanted utterly exposed; they covered only as an invitation to disclose. She was an object, a contrivance entirely got up for the purpose of pursuing sensual pleasure. It was the artifice, the deceit of it she liked so much. The lie that barely concealed itself. The blatant falseness of a notional modesty which left breasts and nipples bra-less and free to be fingered beneath the flimsy silk, and vulva moist and knickerless under the slip, available to any searching hand.

Filled with desire at her image and lusting dreamily for herself, she watched her reflection slide her fingertips lightly down her body, from shoulder to breast, pausing to cup it softly and squeezing her nipple between thumb and finger before continuing down over her rounded belly, and under the pulled-up slip, reaching up between her thighs to part her saturated labia and run her fingers along the length of the valley between them, as silky and smooth as the satin covering her breasts, as slippery and wet as the liver she had donated to the cats. She withdrew her fingers and pressed them against her mouth and nose, taking in the pungent smell of her own desire. "Cunt," she murmured to her image in the mirror, a word only she, it and one other had ever heard her speak. With an approving smile at herself she stroked her damp fingers behind each ear and at the pulse on her neck where normally she dabbed just a little Chanel No. 5. Efficient as always; it was twelve o'clock, and she was ready.

*Sweet Witch, I'm very attached to* more, *too. More and more. This afternoon during a seminar, I remembered (viscerally, that is) the sight of your saliva between your parted lips, and me reaching up to take it from you. "Do you want more?" you asked. And I begged for your saliva, a river of it. "More. More," I said. And you gave me a gift of more and more. So much of you inside me. I wonder if there's a critical dose, after which I am more you than I am me? Or more us than either me or you. I adore your madness and desperately hope no terrible attack of sanity comes over you. I like you mad, my demented Kentish batwitch. You are with me, in that place (in all the places) where you live in me. I'll keep you warm and watered and fed with all the right kind of delicious, dangerous food. Just lie back and enjoy yourself. What else is there for you to do? Or me? We make such fine spells together, what can we be but spellbound? Kiss me, sometimes, when you're alone. I'm hungry to know more of you. I want to hear about your darkness. Whisper some of it to me. I want to be in the dark with you, whispering and playing in the mess of our minds. I miss you. God, the things I want to do to you.*

When Richard arrived, their mouths met like a pair of magnets, too powerfully attracted, too needy to be used for the commonplace of speech. Their tongues greeted each other, instead, investigating their mutual state of desire, while Richard's hand duplicated the exploration Susan's own hand had conducted just a little while before. For a moment they remained like this, sucking in each other's breath, until they had to break apart to take in neutral air. They looked at one another, like people in a state of shock, until Susan smiled a conspiratorial smile.

"You are a filthy bugger," she told him.

"Mmm," he agreed, sucking the taste of her off his fingers and sniffing the air. "You smell of sex."

"You're an animal," she said with desire swimming in her eyes.

He followed her into the bedroom.

"You liked my present, then?"

"Loved it."

He sat on the edge of the bed and Susan straddled him, sitting on his lap with her knees on the bed. He buried his face in her satin cleavage.

"Ahh. I want you," he whispered as she surrounded him with her arms. "I want every morsel of you. I dream about your insides. The thought of your liver has been driving me crazy. In my dreams I try and try to get in there, but I can never get deep enough, never far enough into you."

"Try harder. Keep trying," she said, manoeuvring her naked vulva against his torso. "My liver aches for you to caress it. That is where I want you most of all. Slither through my organs like a serpent. I want your lips brushing against my liver, kissing my spleen. I want your tongue licking around my kidneys. I want you covered in my slime."

"You filthy bitch," he sighed. "Cover me with your stuff."

Susan began to rub herself against his abdomen harder, raising and lowering herself on her knees. He held her tight, nudging one strap off her shoulder to free her breast and take it in his mouth, encouraging her excitement and building on his own, while narrative gave way to the inarticulacy of their moans and then sharp, staccato gasps, like cries of pain.

"You," she breathed between her cries. "Take—everything. All of it. I'm yours."

They made love for an hour, like an overland journey, moving to exhaustion, resting, beginning again with renewed energy. He didn't enter her for a long time; they touched and stroked and mouthed. But each lover made forays into the other's body, boring into each other with fingers and tongue wherever they could be inserted—for her, a foretelling of what was yet to come; for him, penetrated and submissive, as her most willing whore, craving more.

Susan Donahoe was not born to this kind of behaviour. For the greater part of her existence she had lived the life everyone, including herself, had expected of her. Indeed, apart from these afternoons, and at night, when she was lying beside her sleeping husband, she continued to fulfil expectations, and what was more, was pleased to do so. Tom thought of her as a good wife, and the children, when they thought about it at all, considered her a satisfactory mother. And she was happy to be thought of in this way. She was neither resentful of nor frustrated with her lot. Being a mother mattered to her, she loved her children—Corinne and Simon were ten and twelve, well adjusted, normally demanding and enjoyable. She took pride in them. Come to that, she loved Tom and was pleased to hear his key in the door when he got home from work.

It had been her choice to give up her job as a personnel assistant in a department store, to look after the children, and she had no sense of loss, either at the time, or later. On the contrary, her life was full. She had almost completed a degree course in literature with the Open University, and Tom had willingly taken care of the kids when she went off to the summer schools. She planned to continue with her studies, so that by the time the children left home, she would be ready to do a PhD, perhaps on a full-time basis.

She was not aching for anything, as far as she knew. Even the suburban life of Paramount Close was congenial to her. She liked their friends, the dinner parties and Sunday lunches. She enjoyed taking the day off with Margaret, her neighbour, to shop in the West End department stores. The quietness of the Close, its lack of drama, did not dismay her. Susan was no bored housewife. In the evenings, she and Tom discussed his work as a solicitor and what she was reading, as well as keeping a lively conversation going about world events. Neither was radical, but both had found the breath of fresh air of Thatcherdom had soured, and were not sorry to see her go. They were roughly Tory, but *consensus* Tories. "A touch of rising damp," as Tom would joke to their more right-of-centre friends. When Harold Macmillan had spoken with alarm about "selling off the family silver," they had been relieved to hear an old-fashioned, decent Tory view being stated once again.

Susan and Tom had a regular sex life. They slept in a double bed and made love, these days, once or twice a week, and neither of them felt their relationship was anything other than full and successful. Both knew that good marriages found their level over time, and that there was a *great* deal more to the long haul of partnership than fevered sexual activity. When they made love, they satisfied each other, and there was a warmth and familiarity about it which gave both of them pleasure.

Sometimes, as thoughtful people, they worried slightly that life was going so well for them. The Close had seen its share of domestic disruption. The Donahoes, everyone agreed, seemed to have the knack of making domesticity work. Susan knew that, while Tom might have had a passing flirtation or two, he had never been unfaithful to her. She, on her side, had never been unfaithful to Tom, not for fifteen years.

Then, eighteen months ago, at a retirement-cum-Christmas party given for Tom's senior partner, Donald, she had met Richard, Donald's son. Richard was a lecturer in English at a south London poly.

"We're a university now," he smiled at her when they first spoke.

"Who isn't?" she answered.

He was in his mid-thirties—ten years Susan's junior—and married to an aromatherapist called Jackie. They had a small child, Sara, just about to start full-time school. Richard and Susan had talked books and the Open University, where, it turned out, he was a visiting lecturer. He was not particularly striking to look at, his face was pleasant enough though a little nondescript, and he was slightly overweight.

"I'll be seeing you at the summer school," Richard had said pleasantly when she and Tom said goodbye.

*Richard, keep on missing me. Stay obsessed. I dreamed you took me to pieces. Broke into me and cut the threads that hold me together. Then you replaced them with strange extruded stuff (cobwebbed latticework, brittle lace) made of your saliva and kisses. Miracle connective tissue that runs now through my bone marrow and keeps me in one piece, but all the time quivers me on your frequency. I vibrate with you, even when you're not here. Do you know what you do to me, you devious, dirty man? I'm not just yours, I'm made of you. You liquefy me. I have never felt quite so much the sum of my parts, yet at the same time I sense each organ of my body in its right place, doing the right things. I hum with you, through perverse telegraph lines you laid in me when I was distracted. You last in me, not wholly ghost in my machine.*

*Oh, you do distract me. And you aren't good: you're bad, very bad, though saintly in your dedication to the pleasuring of you and me. For which, all must be forgiven. Just now, I conjured you, and you came to me so deliciously, so darkly that I thought, for a moment, that you were really here. Well, you are, of course. I've even come to love the silences between us while we live our other lives, even they speak to me of you.*

*About the things you want to do to me: the answer, so far as my imagination can stretch, and much, much further, is* yes. *What you want—yes. Over and over again. I love repetition.*

*And the things I want to do to you: I want to taste the tears that lubricate your eyes with the tip of my tongue. Your eyelids would resist, but wouldn't be able to prevent my penetration. I'd lick each eye from corner to corner. And then as a prize for being so still, I'd dip my finger into my saturated privates and run it across your mouth. I want to watch your tongue gathering up the taste of me. I'm so happy to be your secret slut, slipping under your skin, into your interior, into the labyrinths where your perverse daydreams huddle. Can you feel me there? In your dark, damp nooks and crannies, nuzzling you and asking for more? I wonder if I should do my PhD in filth? Or limericks. Look, I wrote one for you:*

> A pair who were anal fixated
> Could never entirely be sated
> They weren't just perverse
> It was something much worse
> Even God turned his back when they mated.

Susan had forgotten all about Richard by the time the summer came round. Except, in retrospect, she recalled looking forward to the summer school even more than usual. She was certain, though, that nothing had happened between them at the party, no special looks or anything, and she was sure he had not been on her mind as she packed, with such enthusiasm, for her week at Sussex University.

He was not her tutor, but they found themselves on the first evening sitting in the same group in the bar. They chatted about books, and he moved his stool closer to hers to make their conversation easier above the raised voices of the rest of the crowd, drinking and laughing their way into familiarity. When the others went off to bed, leaving the two of them alone, Susan had not thought anything of it. Even when he walked her back to the hall of residence, and then accompanied her to the door of her room, Susan did not consider it strange or meaningful. It was only when, having unlocked the door and, without a word being spoken, both of them were behind it, in the room, and still in silence they had locked together, fumbling desperately to get each other's clothes off, that Susan realised what was happening.

They never got to the bed, or even fully undressed. He freed her breasts, pulling her blouse and brassiere down to her waist. She opened his flies and, dropping to her knees, grasped inside his underpants to get at his penis and fill her mouth with it, half-choking on its bulk so that the pressure on the back of her throat caused contractions, like swallowing movements, as if she would devour him. In a few moments, he withdrew it, and pressed her down on to the carpet, pushing up her skirt and dragging her knickers to her ankles, only getting one leg free before grasping both breasts between his fingers, and entering her. He drove himself into her, tightening his grip on her nipples with every movement, and spitting the word, "Fuck! Fuck! Fuck!" into her face, and although she had no recollection of ever before using the word, she called it back to him with matching ferocity, until the two of them were so fiercely in unison that suddenly they both laughed out loud. He kissed her then, and the laughter died as his tongue reached towards the back of her throat, tasting her and himself at the same time, and he came with a cry that travelled down from the interior of Susan's mouth into her abdomen and brought her to an anguished and frighteningly strange orgasm of her own.

In the ensuing silence, they were strangers in shock: people meeting for the first time in the aftermath of a natural catastrophe, not knowing how to address each other once the intimacy of disaster was over. Someone moved slightly, Susan did not know who, and it cued their separation. Hesitantly, rather awkwardly, Richard kissed her on the lips, but it had about it the quality of a well-mannered gesture. You had to do something to recognise the person you barely knew, when you had just had tumultuous sex with them. She knew he would rather have dressed himself in silence and left, because that was what she wanted to do. It wasn't that she felt that either of them disliked the other for what had happened, only that it was such an embarrassing situation they now found themselves in.

Neither of them found appropriate words—not surprisingly on Susan's part, she didn't know what they were, she had never done anything like this before. They dressed, turning their backs on each other for modesty, and then stood in the vacant silence.

"I'd better go. I'm . . ." Richard said. She could hear that he had been about to add an apology, but decided against it, not wanting it to be misunderstood.

"Yes," she said, meaning nothing very much at all.

Again, at the open door, Richard turned as if to say something, feeling, Susan knew, that he ought to arrange another meeting, that it was not right to leave it like this; but instead he cracked a bit of a smile and closed the door behind him with elaborate care.

They continued to see each other in the bar, but never when there wasn't a group of other students and teachers around them. There was no remaining behind when the evening's socialising was done. When they passed each other on the way to lectures, he gave her a fleeting smile that suggested he remembered what had happened, but could not cope with anything more than that. Susan's smile said the same thing. If it had been an adventure, it was one which both were happy to leave to find its place in the past.

A month later, he phoned her in the middle of the day.

"I want to see you," he said. Just that, no greeting or explanation.

"All right," Susan replied, and he arranged to come to her house at midday the following day.

They fucked immediately on Susan and Tom's bed, as frantically as they had at the summer school, but this time they continued to lie in each other's arms. When they'd rested in an easier and far more comfortable silence than after their first encounter, they began again, but now it was different, and they took their time, exploring their faces and bodies with delicate care, watching the response to every slight caress. They called each other by name, tentatively at first, and looked into each other's eyes to judge the pleasure they were giving and convey the pleasure they were receiving.

After that he came to her twice a week, on the days when his timetable left him free before and after lunch. It was, to Susan's surprise, extraordinarily easy to push past the limits of what she had once considered to be generally acceptable. The exploration of the boundaries—physical and mental—between them became the structure of their affair. On his second visit, while Richard moved slowly, thoughtfully inside her, Susan's hand casually stroked his lower back and continued around the curve of his buttock. As a sudden spasm of desire ran through her, she gripped him harder, her fingers digging into the dividing slope, and for a split second the rhythm of his movements was interrupted. She looked up at him and saw some new longing in his eyes. That time, the moment passed, and they continued their slow and sensual reacquaintance, but Susan took note.

Each time they met, they tested the further possibilities of what was wanted of them and by them, and each time found they had not reached the innermost boundary of desire. When, cued by the look in his eyes on the previous occasion, she first penetrated him with her finger, he moaned and abandoned himself readily to her exploration. He breathed "Yes," as if he had been waiting for it, and lay wide open and shuddering with an almost deranged pleasure at feeling himself invaded and caressed so deep inside his body. She discovered a new sense of power, a novel potency which made her heart beat fast and her eyes gleam, while she released his desire to be taken and used.

The increasing reification of each other's body became a goal and a gift. Her body was put at the disposal of his every whim, to be his object with which he could do anything he chose, and she saw how he, too, wanted the pure physicality of being reduced (though this was not how either experienced it) to a sexual commodity. She had never felt so much *herself* as when she was utterly and explicitly his object, a thing with no other use than to gratify his impulses. Nor had she known such welling passion, and what she would have called love if it had not been so much more and different a matter from the love she felt for Tom, as when her existence was being annihilated by his unfettered desire to have *everything* of her. They were possessed by one another and the desire for total possession of the other's body. Very quickly, it was clear that everything was allowed and wanted. But soon enough they'd reached the limits of the physically possible and they discovered they were not satiated. Their desire surpassed the accessible areas of their bodies.

Richard wanted to know, one day, who got up first in Susan's house, who collected the post? The following morning the first letter arrived. When they met a couple of days later, they smiled at one another, but made no mention of their exchange of letters. The story they were weaving by post continued in parallel to their meetings.

And so it went on, almost daily by post, and twice a week, in reality. They detailed their daydreams on paper and without any sense of hurry, though with studied compulsion, acted them out on the flesh. They delighted and amused each other with the games they invented, the roles they played in both their modes of communication. They encouraged each other, urging each other on to go deeper into their desires, to say what had never been said, to wish for what couldn't be wished for, to do whatever they liked.

Yet, all the while, life went on as normal. The families noticed very little change; nothing more than a slightly distracted air from time to time. Tom would smile when Susan failed to hear something he said while she sat and read a book in the evening.

"Too immersed in her studies to hear her poor old husband," he joked at her on that evening when the two cats were lying purring at their feet, fat and sleek after a large liver lunch. Tom was pleased to have a wife with a lively intelligence.

"Mmm," she said, looking up briefly, and smiling back.

*Susan, my Sidcup siren, let me tutor you in your PhD. I promise to give you very high marks, you'll be a doctor of filth in no time, so long as you promise never to cure me. God, I wish I could mark you, and you me. It's impractical, I know, but I long to trace the outlines of the bruises you would leave on me. The maps of pain and pleasure I know you know how to give. And your blood—what would it taste like?*

*It's funny about the silences, isn't it? But I love your sound and your presence, even more. I want to be drip-fed with your voice, your words. Even then, I'd fret when you took the time to breathe. I have such a need for you, such a hunger, and yet I want us to take our time. I want to go through in the flesh everything we're going through in the story we've been telling each other by post (and the other, even murkier story which we haven't dared commit to words: too dangerous), but slowly, deliberately. I want to kiss you for an age and toy with time.*

*I could swear that you are my invention. How else could you be how you are? I worked on your wishes just as I work on your body, making them real and solid. You are a monster conceived out of my own monstrous desires, for all your pretty floral curtains and blu-flush in the loo. But we're angelic monsters, not fiends. The fiends couldn't stand the heat we create.*

*The project of inventing you is going so well, though it's slow, careful work. (Sometimes, Susan, I'm so scared about us, I can hardly breathe.) I'm starting from the inside: building from the centre and working out. (I don't want us to stop. I want to go on. Is it OK?) I've got your delicious entrails in place, and they're very beautiful, I wish you could see them. Soon, I'll have your major organs mapped. Oh, I can't wait to get to your bloodstream. I'll carry on working on you for the rest of the evening. Tomorrow is dedicated to inventing your lungs and spleen. The next day I think I'll devote entirely to your heart.*

*People don't understand about repetition, do they? How it is at the heart (thump, thump, thump) of obsession; at the erotic centre (drip, drip, drip) of desire. You do, of course. Repetition is insatiability spelt sideways.*

*I love your ability to focus. Apart from repetition, focus is the main requirement of good obsessives. You are such a good obsessive. Do you know that, sometimes, when I see the word "you" in one of your letters, my heart stops for a moment?*

*My turn:*

> A batwitch who rode through the night
> On a bookish young man did alight
> She unleashed all her passion
> In unspeakable fashion
> When he thanked her, she said "That's all right."

In between lusting and family life, the subject of betrayal did, of course, occupy Susan's thoughts. She knew that she was betraying Tom by any common definition of fidelity, but was she, she wondered, betraying Richard's wife? This question engaged her for some time, seeming, at least at first, to be a different matter from her infidelity to Tom.

Richard had told her that he had had a couple of affairs during his five-year marriage, before his involvement with Susan, and it was clear to her right from the start that Richard was not a man who would be faithful to a wife. She was fairly certain that "a couple of affairs" meant more than two. She argued to herself that he would be sleeping with someone else if he were not sleeping with her. This was a statement of the particular situation, rather than a justification for her affair with a married man, but Susan discovered that she simply did not feel guilt about Jackie the aromatherapist. That marriage was entirely their concern: she did not discuss it with Richard, and would not talk about Jackie, even in passing.

"Why?" he asked when she stopped him telling her something Jackie had said about sending their daughter to private school.

"Because if Tom was in bed with another woman, whatever I felt about his infidelity, I wouldn't want him chatting to her about me. It doesn't matter what's said. Your wife has a right to privacy. She's none of my business."

"You think the injustice to her is any less if we don't mention her name?"

"I don't know about the injustice to her. That's also for the two of you."

Richard privately thought this was a pretty thin way to deny her own responsibility. But Susan, for whatever motive, developed a rational view of her relationship with Jackie's husband. What went on between them occurred, so far as she was concerned, in a vacuum which had nothing to do with his wife and family. Only if she intended or wanted to intervene, to break up their marriage, would she be participating in their family life. And she had no such intention, no such desire. She saw herself as harmless and neutral in relation to Jackie. When she and Richard met, it was during his working time, never when he might otherwise be at home, and she was clear that, astonishing and thrilling though their relationship was to both of them, it didn't impinge on Richard's marriage. She was providing an alternative sexuality, and Richard loved his family; these were two unconnected facts. He was not dissatisfied and looking for somewhere else to go. Jackie was family; Susan was fantasy. They were separate things. Therefore there was no cause for the guilt which, however much she tested for it, she did not feel.

"Do you do what we do, with your wife?" she asked when he questioned her argument for practical innocence.

"Never," he told her, quite shocked at the idea. "It wouldn't come up. I'm not unhappy with our sex life. It's quiet but very good. I wouldn't want it different."

Susan had no difficulty understanding this and it satisfied her own reasoning.

The fact was, however, that betrayal of Jackie was very close to the centre of Richard's and Susan's activities together. For Richard, Susan knew quite consciously, his good marriage with Jackie *had* to be betrayed in order to remain good. Infidelity was essential as a balance to Richard's loving-husband role, it was the culture in which their marriage survived, and she suspected that Jackie knew something of it, perhaps choosing to remain silent as her part of the good-marriage bargain. If Jackie was not betrayed, she would have had to take on the sinful Richard who was not a good husband and responsible father. Better for that Richard to remain outside the domestic sphere. Indeed, Susan sometimes felt, in relation to Jackie, that she was providing her with an essential service. Another woman might demand more of Richard than his sexual obsession. Richard and Jackie's marriage was safe in Susan's hands.

But there was also an aspect of her affair which Susan did not so readily confront. There was Susan's own separate and particular betrayal not just, obviously, of Tom, but, in truth, of Jackie as well. It was a betrayal which was not related to Richard's agenda at all. Consciously and socially, Susan had no wish to bring Jackie into her affair; but half-consciously and sexually, Richard's wife was fully, if subtextually (as her English tutor would say), present. There was a *frisson* she rarely chose to define, but which was ever-present in her passion during her love-making with Richard, written and performed. It was Susan's thrill at her awareness of The Wife's ignorance of what her husband was up to at that moment—*at this very moment*—with her. Often the image of Jackie (just glimpsed at the Christmas party), working away in her white coat on some pampered body, or in her car, driving the child to school, would surface, while Richard was expressing excruciated pleasure at what Susan was doing to him with her hands or tongue. Her own orgasms were enhanced by the fleeting glimpse of an oblivious Jackie peeling the potatoes for supper.

Eventually, Susan could no longer suppress her knowledge of how much Jackie's ignorance and betrayal added to her excitement. She admitted to herself that her enhanced pleasure at the deceit of her affair made her, by any standards, not a nice person, but she found herself surprised (and perhaps a little relieved) rather than distressed at this discovery of her true nature.

She never voiced anything of this to Richard, but again it was not because she felt ashamed. On the contrary, her silence provided a double gratification: not only the original deceit against The Wife, but also the dishonesty of her dialogue on Jackie's rights with Richard, which amounted to a secret betrayal of her lover as well as Jackie. She cherished the silent lies that lived only in her heart. She suspected it was the same for Richard, though she had no wish to share her insight with him. She did not believe that he got no pleasure from the fact of his infidelity to Jackie. His protestations that he loved his wife differently though deeply and therefore was not betraying her were the same lies that she told and created for him, she supposed; the same private multiple pleasure in deceit that she experienced. And then, of course, there was her own husband. The spare bedroom in their house, with its made-up bed, might have been designed for an illicit afternoon affair, but Susan always led Richard to the bed she and Tom slept in every night to fuck him.

With everyone who was not her deceived and ignorant of her unfaithfulness to them, Susan had created a secret and secluded pool of pleasure to dip into which was for no one but herself. It felt necessary to her, as if some essential part of her was strengthened—fed and nurtured into solidity—by her solipsistic knowledge. It was not that she wanted anyone's pain, not at all, only that she wanted to enjoy the benefits of a sequestered Elysium that was hers alone, and which added no actual suffering to anyone's life, as far as she could see.

She did not transform this into a moral somersault and consider herself ethically justified. She understood quite clearly the moral position which declared that people were injured just by being betrayed; that broken trust was betrayal whether it was exposed or not. Innocent parties did not have to participate in the infidelity by their knowledge of it to be the victims of it.

But she was not taking a moral position. She did not *feel* the moral position to be the slightest burden on her conscience. Mrs. Donahoe, suburban housewife and mother, contributor to the profits of Marks & Spencer and John Lewis, Parent Governor of

Sidcup Junior School, practising owner of the Delia Smith wipe clean cookery cards, found herself to be a woman without the faintest remnants of a conscience, and she was considerably surprised. Try as she might, she could find no guilt, towards anybody, about her behaviour. She required no forgiveness, for she had not the faintest sense that there was anything to forgive. Unconsciously, surely? Well, how would she know? She slept well enough and lived through her days without the slightest difficulty. The situation pleased her in its entirety. She had no hankerings to sabotage it by confessing anything to anyone, or leaving clues as to her guilt. She was meticulous about changing the sheets, airing the bedroom, and showering the scent of Richard off her body before the children and Tom returned to the house. There were no accidental Freudian absent-mindednesses that put her affair at risk. All the parts of her life seemed to be working fine.

"Big case next month in Lewes. I think I'm going to have to stay there for a week or so."

Susan looked up from her book, this time, giving her husband her full attention.

"When?"

"Second week, definitely, and possibly into the third. Will you manage all right?"

"Of course I will," she told him. "Anyway, I owe you some time from the summer school."

"I don't think about it like that," Tom said, feeling hurt.

"Oh, no, of course you don't. I didn't mean it like that. Really, it's all right. It's not even school holidays."

It had been a while since Tom spent time away from home on business, but every now and then a case came up which he felt was important enough to need to be there throughout.

"I was thinking," Tom added, with a smile that wrinkled

the corners of his eyes, "when I get back, why don't we take the kids to my mother, and spend the weekend in the country? A nice break. Treat for us both."

Susan looked pleased. She was pleased.

"That's a lovely idea. Book it up. Somewhere quiet with very good food, darling."

She could tell they would be making love tonight. This pleased her, too.

The following day Richard arrived at twelve o'clock. After they had lain sweating in each other's exhausted embrace for a while, Susan spoke.

"Tom's going away for a week next month."

"Oh? But you'll have the kids won't you?"

Susan detected slight alarm in his voice. Did he think she was going to ask for a whole night together? Or more?

"Do you remember what you said in one of your letters, about wishing you had the marks on you we can't make because it would be indiscreet?"

He looked at her half-sexual, half-anxious.

"Jackie isn't going away."

"I want what you want. Remember how our dreams fit on top of each other. A bruise or two, or marks on my wrists from a tight knot . . . they'd be gone by the time Tom came back."

Richard's anxiety flew away.

"Whore," he whispered in delight.

"Your whore. I've got a selection of scarves you can use."

"What are they made of?" Richard's voice was curiously husky.

"What difference does it make what they're made of?" Susan laughed.

"Silk chiffon is best, though a slightly rough, silky viscose does nicely, too."

Susan rested on her elbow and stared, amused and excited, into her lover's face.

"Tell me."

"I use scarves sometimes on my own."

"Your wife's scarves? To do what?"

"My scarves. I keep a small collection in my room at college. When I'm alone I use them to masturbate."

"*Tell* me," Susan insisted.

"I've never told anyone about it before."

"Tell *me*! *Tell* me!"

"There's a way of tying them, it's incredibly—exciting . . ." He was a little abashed. Not certain what reaction he would get.

"Details. I want details, please."

"Well, I tie one side around my waist, and then hook the remainder hanging down the back—it's got to be a long scarf—between my buttocks . . . and then you spread it out over your balls and cock."

"*Your* balls and cock."

"You're very strict. *My* cock and balls—which I stroke, very slowly, through the material—God, you've got no idea how it feels—and, as an extra treat, while I'm stroking, I hold the loose end with my other hand . . ."

Susan jumped out of bed and began rummaging about in her closet.

"It's no good, I've got no visual imagination. Does the colour matter? Show me."

She whisked out a couple of long silk chiffon scarves and threw them across to Richard where they settled on him like fairy clocks blown by the wind.

"You aren't bothered by my confession, then?"

"No, I'm thrilled. Richard, you must tell me everything. Every detail of your desires. I'm going to take all your secrets."

He took a scarf and knelt on the bed, tying it around himself as he had described. He was as efficient and practised as a man doing up his tie. All the while, Susan lay along the foot of the bed and kept her eyes unblinkingly on his activity. He watched her watching him doing what no one had ever witnessed before. When he was ready, he lay back on the bed and began to stroke himself. Susan kept her eyes fixed on him while she took the second scarf and, wrapping it around her waist, draped it between her parted legs. She ran her fingers softly over the fabric.

"Here, let me tie it properly for you."

Richard stopped and tied her scarf around her so that she had a similar tension between her buttocks and could manipulate the loose end with her free hand to increase the pressure.

"Oh, Richard," Susan whispered, and while working gently on herself, reached out to do for him what he was doing himself.

"Is that good? Is that how you like it?"

He reached out to her, and they worked on each other until Richard moved towards her.

"Keep the scarves between us," Susan whispered as she opened her legs to receive him, and they made love between two layers of chiffon, chaffing sweetly and pulling against the tenderest places on their bodies and into climaxes quite beyond anything they had ever known before.

"I wish I could keep the smell of us on them," Susan said when they'd finished, gathering up the scarves for washing. "When Tom's away, we'll have to use something else to tie me to the bed, so we can get them in this state again and I won't have to wash them. I can sleep with them on my pillow for a week, my love, my lover, my whore."

Richard lay astonished at his good fortune in finding the mirror of his dreams. He wanted to hold her tightly and tell her he loved her, which was true, though only in a way specific to her. He was almost sure she would understand, but she had gone into the bathroom and was running the shower for the washing of the scarves and their bodies back to respectability.

"And you," Richard said, soaping her in the shower. "I want your secrets. All of them."

"Of course you do. They're yours. My plans for when Tom's away: they're much more detailed. I'll write to you about them—with details and exact instructions as to how you are to be my master. And you'll follow them to the letter, won't you?"

"Of course, I'm your slave," he said, and bent to bite her breast, but gently enough not to show any marks.

"I love you," she said, taking his wet head between her hands and pulling him close against her breasts.

He knew exactly what she meant.

"Nice meal," said Tom, scraping up the last of the raspberry *coulis*.

"Delicious. And we've got a whole day and night to go."

"Breakfast in bed, tomorrow."

"Late breakfast in bed," Susan hummed.

"Mmm," Tom agreed. "Mustn't miss lunch, though."

"We might," she said, with a smile.

"Yes, we might," her husband agreed, wiping his mouth and pushing back his chair. "Come on, time for bed, old thing. Not feeling too sleepy, I hope?"

Susan shook her head, dreamy with good food and wine. She knew exactly what he meant.

# Strictempo

*Dancing in the dark*
*Till the tune ends*
*We're dancing in the dark*
*And it soon ends*
*We're waltzing in the wonder of why we're here*
*Time hurries by; we're here*
*Then we're gone . . .*

Hannah slid around the polished floor in the arms of her partner, trying to follow as smoothly as he led. Her arm ached because Terry was much taller than her, and it meant that her right hand was held in his at a very awkward angle. She hoped she was doing the right steps. She had learned to do the quickstep—side, side, step behind—at ballroom dancing classes at school, but once rock 'n' roll impinged on her consciousness she'd given up, so she never learned to foxtrot. But Terry had medals, bronze, silver *and* gold, for ballroom dancing, and he used his body to signal to Hannah what she should do next, gently pushing her ahead of him. As long as she didn't try to think about it, she made the right moves, or enough of them to allow Terry to manoeuvre her around the floor without either of them looking too foolish.

Of course, she felt foolish anyway. What fourteen-year-old in 1962 would not flush as pink as her layered net petticoat with embarrassment at doing ballroom dancing in public? Luckily, there was no one of her own age to see her. She was humiliated only in her own eyes.

Dances happened once a week, on Friday nights. The rug on the dayroom floor was rolled away to reveal polished wood that was perfect for dancing. The chairs and low tables were already ranged around the edges of the room. Danny was in charge of the record player. Reading from the record sleeves, he would announce the next dance.

"Right, it's a samba. Let's make this a Ladies' Excuse Me. Of *course* we'll excuse you, ladies, we know you can't help it."

Danny was very outgoing, which made him a natural choice for master of ceremonies. Not that anyone had chosen him; he just took charge of social activities, and no one else wanted to do it.

The music was mostly provided by three LPs called *Sinatra Sings Strictempo, Volumes 1 to 3*, which were special dance tempo arrangements of Frank's best-known songs. Once or twice during the Social, Danny would announce, "Right, now, specially for the wild teenagers in this establishment, it's . . . the Twist!"

He tried to sound enthusiastic, but his heart wasn't really in it. Danny was only in his early thirties, but he liked a decent tune, with a proper rhythm, and a singer who could sing. Hannah was the only teenager in the hospital but, in fact, almost everybody danced to the Chubby Checker records she had asked her father to send. Everybody, that is, who danced at all. But even the patients who sat in their chairs all evening seemed to enjoy watching the energetic gyrations of the more active inmates, and were to be seen tapping their feet.

Nonetheless, it was with something like relief that Danny announced, "Right-oh, Pop-pickers, that's your lot. Back to good ol' Frank."

It was in the hospital that Hannah discovered she could dance. Not the ballroom stuff, which was a matter of getting the steps right, but the Twist. She hadn't mixed much with people of her own age for some time, so she didn't normally go to dances. Even when she was at school, she didn't dance. She wasn't popular, and didn't have a boyfriend, so during the dances she stood with a few other loners against the wall because only girls with boyfriends were asked to dance. Then she'd stopped bothering to go, telling herself that dancing, like sport, was for idiots.

But having contributed Chubby Checker and her two Elvis singles to the hospital record collection, she was committed to dancing to them, and lo and behold, it turned out she did the Twist like a dream, and, with Terry, who was older, she jived everyone off the floor. The first time, everyone stopped dancing and stood in a circle around her, clapping and cheering her on, as if she were in a film. It surprised Hannah to find that she could dance, but there was no doubt that she had a natural sense of rhythm, and moved with a freedom that she didn't possess in normal circumstances. Secretly, from then on, she looked forward to the Friday Social. She liked being able to do something physical with ease, and she discovered she also liked being watched. She knew she danced all the better for having an admiring audience.

Part of her still thought that, in a way, dancing was for fools, especially when she watched the patients shuffling around the dayroom every Friday during the therapeutically approved Social. Anyone who was mobile was chivvied by the staff into going downstairs. They went from ward to ward turfing people out, even looking in cupboards for the more extreme unsociable types. There was always one cupboard with an unwilling socialite in it. The Social was supposed to be good for everyone: practice at joining in and being part of the larger community. It reminded Hannah, when she was not dancing herself, of the Caucus race in *Alice in Wonderland.* Round and round the room—always clockwise—they all went for the allotted two hours, as though they thought that if they went round enough times they'd break out of the circle and dance off into the real world. But Hannah knew by now that the real world was the last place most of them wanted to be, and the going round and round was actually a reassurance, or a kind of magical rite they hoped would keep them within the safe confines of the walls. Still, there was nothing else to do on a Friday evening, and, as long as Hannah felt no one *outside* saw her, she joined in with her teeth only slightly gritted. In fact, rather than singers of the acceptable peer-group taste, she loved Sinatra's voice, the melodies of the songs he sang and, most of all, the lyrics.

It seemed to Hannah that she had been going round in circles for ever, but this particular circle had been going on for only six months. It just seemed like an eternity. Funny things happen to time in the Bin. She had been there for four months. Before that she had been in her mother's room for two days. Before that she had been in Banbury with her father for two months. And before that . . .

*Let's take it nice and easy*
*It's gonna be so easy*
*For us to fall in love*
*Hey baby what's your hurry*

*Relax and don't you worry*
*We're gonna fall in love*
*The problem now of course is*
*To simply hold your horses*
*To rush would be a crime*
*'Cos nice and easy does it every time*

Two weeks after Hannah's fifteenth birthday she sat, silently, in the headmaster's study while he told her that he would have to ask her to leave. For a moment Hannah toyed with the idea of saying no, since he asked, on the whole she thought she wouldn't. But she'd been at the school for long enough to know the code. This was a liberal, progressive, vegetarian boarding school where self-government and rational discourse were the golden rules by which all members of the community were supposed to live. So punishments were known as "the consequences of one's actions," prefects were called "servers," and "being asked to leave" meant that Hannah had been expelled.

A dogged air of reason hung heavily about the place, and it was supposed to go without saying that individuals of any age responded rationally to rational treatment. *Or else*, as was now apparent. If smugness were asphyxiating, you could have died of it there.

Hannah knew there was no point in arguing with facts, however conveyed, and she certainly wasn't going to give Nicholas, the Head (they were on democratic, first-name terms with the staff) the impression that she cared.

"All right," she said, "I will."

"I called your father and told him I could no longer accept responsibility for you after noon today. Unfortunately, he's moving this weekend and can't come to get you. I said I would keep you here until Monday, and put you on the train."

This was Friday. Hannah saw her chance.

"You've given up responsibility for me from midday. I'm not your concern after that. I've got a friend I can stay with in town, and there's a party I planned to go to tomorrow night."

It was a party Hannah had been to the previous night which was the cause of her present situation.

According to the school gossip, Nicholas had really wanted to be a lawyer, but he had done his familial duty and taken over the school when his father died. He nodded seriously at the logic of Hannah's argument, in spite of its obvious legal incorrectness. He was also, of course, swayed by the potential disruption of having an already expelled Hannah rattling round the school all weekend.

He agreed to let her go, provided he could talk to the parent of the friend she planned to stay with, and if she promised to leave the party at midnight. (Nicholas never lost his faith in promises and reasonable requests—the following summer he was killed while on holiday in Gibraltar, run down by a lorry driving in the wrong direction down the one-way street he was cycling along.)

Hannah did leave the party at midnight, a strict attention to honour she would always regret on principle.

When she left Nicholas' study, his secretary stopped her.

"We phoned your mother to ask her if she could take you, since your father wouldn't. She said no. No one wants you, do they?"

Hannah just stared at her. Only later did she decide that the secretary must have been suffering hopeless love for her boss, and that that, rather than personal hatred, caused her to say what she did.

All in all, it was a pretty miserable weekend. Hannah had come seriously adrift. She had always relied until then on her proven capacity for survival to take her to the brink of disaster but no further. She hadn't really imagined that anything so final would happen.

It was a kind of paradise, that school situated a mile or so from the garden city of Letchworth. It spread itself comfortably over several acres. Unmade paths (pitted with potholes that the pupils had to fill at weekends when their actions required consequences) linked the rambling country houses where they lived with the main teaching block, set around an old stone courtyard. There was an orchard just behind it where, if the weather was fine, Reg would conduct his Philosophy of Religion classes. But the trees, part of a system of organic gardening, though full of fruit, seemed only to bear wormy apples. One especially sunny day, Reg arrived with a great basket of cream cakes and distributed them among Hannah's class. He said he'd wanted one himself, but couldn't have borne to eat it while watching their yearning, junk-food-hungry faces gazing up at him. The vegetables in the organic garden next to the orchard grew on in silent disapproval, as Hannah's form briefly raised their cholesterol levels and deepened their understanding of the Buddhist way. But as Hannah remembered the occasion later, in the hospital, and could almost taste the choux pastry melting with the whipped cream in her mouth, she was no longer certain that it had happened. She thought, perhaps, that the cream cakes were only ever promised—a tantalising joke—and that the virtue of the organic vegetables was never in serious jeopardy.

Beyond the orchard was the neatly mown and rolled playing field, laid out for cricket, lacrosse and football; and beyond that was a meadow which, though strictly speaking not school property, was very much the pupils' territory. Courting couples and smokers, released from the day's lessons, wandered into, and then disappeared beneath, the thigh-deep grass and wild flowers. From a distance their position could be spotted by the plumes of forbidden smoke that spiralled up into the air, like the camps of so many Indians, signalling to one another.

It was idyllic, as Hannah remembered it.

Of course, she hated the compulsory cold bath and morning walk before breakfast, especially on frozen winter mornings when her curses took on visible form in front of her face. And she had never been able to summon enthusiasm for muesli. A decade later, it might look neat and healthy in pretty earthenware bowls on the modern breakfast table, but at school it came by the gallon in vast tin vats, copiously wet and thick, waiting to be slopped into the pupils' plates and given a good stir every now and then with a giant metal spoon so that the repellently plump raisins were distributed fairly throughout the dreadful, glutinous mess.

It certainly wouldn't have looked, to an outsider, as if Hannah would remember her time at the school as idyllic. She took the precepts of self-government and maintaining a questioning attitude to life as far as she could. She joined the school council and proposed wild (and probably illegal) motions, which were passed, and then, on the informed advice of the Head, expunged from the minutes. She refused to participate in the dangerous madness of lacrosse, laid down her stick and sat, a precursor of Bertrand Russell, in the middle of the pitch until the games teacher called the Head, who thereafter drove Hannah out into the countryside at the beginning of each games period and left her to find her way back in time for English. As she trudged across the fields smoking the cigarettes she had stuffed up her knickers, she had the uneasy feeling that whoever had won the battle, it hadn't been her. She took down every other line of the notes the physics teacher wrote on the board, and turned them into poems about parallax; and maths classes were held up while she demanded to know why she should accept that parallel lines meet at infinity. So what if it was axiomatic? What if it wasn't true anyway?

But until she started climbing out of the dormitory window to attend midnight parties, nothing more dramatic happened than a look of weariness and the suggestion from Hannah's tutor that she might channel some of her energies into joining the debating society.

Finally, though, she found a way to get to them.

She had returned to school that term after a particularly angry Easter at home, determined to be bad. She made a clear and conscious decision as she stood in the rattling corridor of the train, hating the place she was leaving behind, but knowing also that she wasn't going to get what she wanted from where she was heading. So far she'd been awkward and difficult but remained within the ethos of the school. And then it came to her, like a revelation, that going too far was a territorial concept. It was a matter, literally, of going beyond the school bounds. It never seemed to matter greatly what was going on in the meadow where the couples sank out of sight and the puffs of smoke rose, so long as it was going on between members of the school. As in a properly constituted family, what went on, discreetly, between themselves was tolerated. Outsiders, even the partial outsiders, were another thing. There were some non-boarders at the school, but they had to be off the premises once the school day was over, and the local town was off-limits without written slips and a good reason. Being caught in the town without an exeat was a serious offence.

So Hannah began to spend most of her free time there, in a coffee bar which had just opened. The new coffee bars, with their hissing, foreign-sounding machines and drinks—Gaggias, espressos—and their rock'n'roll-filled jukeboxes, were notoriously the first step on the recently invented teenagers' rocky road to ruin. Once or twice Hannah was seen through the steam-clouded window by a passing teacher and the warning she received confirmed that she was taking the right route.

She met Bob, five years older than herself, and a trainee reporter on the local paper. He had read a little Kerouac and Burroughs and pressed copies of *Jude the Obscure* and *Ulysses* on Hannah. She and Bob blew smoke at each other across their cappuccinos as they discussed despair and Raskolnikov. Very existential, and a perfect fit for Hannah's own private sense of doom. They set each other stories to write that had to begin: "The chair hated the table . . ." and they mulled over the novel Bob planned to write when he wasn't so tied up with reporting council meetings and weddings; it was to be five hundred pages long and span five minutes of the hero's life. And she climbed out of windows and down drainpipes late at night to join him and his friends in their celebrations of the human predicament, which, like most other parties, consisted of cider and heavy petting, although, for reasons Hannah couldn't fathom, they never quite succeeded in going the whole way.

None of this was radically different from what was on offer at school. It was possible, most weekends, if you were in with the right people, to sneak out of the dormitory and attend a huddled gathering in one of the huts dotted around the playing field that served as rooms for some of the sixth-form boys. And, in all likelihood, both Hardy and Joyce were freely available in the school library. But the fact that Bob was *not* from the school was crucial. They knew it and so did Hannah. She'd found a place she felt she belonged that was neither school nor home, and what was more, she was accepted. If it also breached the fundamental, unspoken rules, then so much the better.

Until, that is, she was caught returning in time for breakfast, happy and tired, from that last party, and she was out, firmly and for good. The limbo weekend was a prelude to going home, and that was not a happy prospect.

For a year before going to the school she had been living with her father and stepmother, locked in a grim and silent battle. Her stepmother was a plain, hard-working and, to Hannah, mysteriously Protestant woman who had been diligent and dutiful all her life. She had brought up a family on her own when her first husband deserted her, and ran a newsagent's that required her to be up and busy by five every morning, seven days a week. She always wore one of those dull, flowery, sleeveless overalls that slipped over her ordinary clothes and tied firmly at the waist, as if to emphasise her commitment to the virtue of persistent hard work. Her lips seemed perpetually pursed and quivering with self-righteousness. Now, in middle age, she found herself, improbably, the companion of choice of Hannah's ageing and tired, but still handsome and, to her, debonair, father. She devoted herself to maintaining his comfort and continued presence with further drudgery and was less than delighted when Hannah arrived: insolent, angry and bent on winning back her vanished-but-now-found father. For his part, her father sat at the still centre of the rivalry, wondering wistfully if he shouldn't write his memoirs. "After all," he would say from the depths of the chintz-covered armchair he had substituted for excitement, "there's nothing Errol Flynn did that I haven't done."

The social workers and shrinks who by now were hovering over the dysfunctional family could see that no good was going to come of this arrangement, and since returning to the volatile mother Hannah had run away from was deemed out of the question, they decided to send her to the school, which took a small number of council "cases," and where, it was hoped, the liberal, progressive atmosphere would suit Hannah.

Well, now they knew. And Hannah had wondered on the train home what Banbury was like (the previous Friday being the first she'd heard of their move from London), and what kind of schools the town had.

She needn't have bothered. Hannah's stony-faced father met her at the station and took a deep, chest-expanding breath as they walked to the car.

"I've done a lot of bad things in my time, Hannah, that I should regret." He had, and some of them not entirely unconnected with the predicament Hannah now found herself in. "But I was never sacked from school. Now, you earn your living like everyone else. I've got you a job locally. You start tomorrow."

So education was at an end, and, though this was unexpected, Hannah supposed that if one jumped off the edge of a cliff, one had no right to be surprised at anything one might find at the bottom.

She went to work the next morning at Cullens the grocers, filling the shelves and packing orders into cardboard boxes. It wasn't altogether unpleasant; for one thing, they roasted their own coffee and the fumes of the best Arabica filled the air deliciously.

Since Hannah wasn't speaking to anyone in the house, nor they to her, she spent a lot of her time wondering. When she wasn't filling shelves, she lay on her bed in the spare room in the attic and wondered why it was that Lolita, silly girl, didn't appreciate Humbert, and how it was that Radio Luxembourg always faded to a crackle whenever they played a record she liked, and whether there really were more spiders in her room than anywhere else in the world, and what was going to happen.

The first thing that happened was that she got the sack again. It wasn't anything she'd done especially, more a matter of attitude and facial expression. The former being about not taking the initiative fast enough when goods needed replacing on the shelves; the latter, more decisive, fault being the greater problem. Not looking as if she minded about anything required an internal organisation of her facial muscles to keep everything light and steady, but the external manifestation of this internal effort tended to bring the word "belligerent" to the furious lips of those who scanned the language to explain the anger Hannah engendered in them. Anyway, that was what the manager said, that he didn't like the belligerent look on her face and she shouldn't bother to return on Monday.

On Monday, thanks to her father's efforts to keep her employed, she began work selling shoes at Freeman, Hardy and Willis. She quite enjoyed it, and although she missed the smell of fresh-roasted coffee, she discovered a new pleasure in the scent of leather. She particularly enjoyed the tea-breaks, when she gossiped with her fellow sales assistant, who (though she seemed fairly old to Hannah) was about twenty-eight. What interested Hannah most were her tales of married life. It seemed that after nine years of what was apparently a happy marriage her husband had never, not once, seen her naked. She undressed in the bathroom and they "did it" under the bedclothes with the lights off. This was the first grown-up sex Hannah had heard about (apart from the dirty bits in *Lady Chatterley* she'd tried to make head or tail of at school) and she was amazed.

"Never? Not once?" she'd ask, thinking how difficult it must be to arrange in a small council flat.

"Well, it's not nice, is it?"

The other assistant found Hannah just as odd: the peculiar school she'd been to, *and* expelled, and Hannah had confided to her that what she really wanted to do when she grew up, as she still thought of it, was to be a writer.

They found each other very interesting.

But it was that last confidence that did it. The manager had overheard them talking and later in the day Hannah was called into his office.

"We took you on as a trainee. There's a lot to learn about this business. I'm afraid you haven't been quite honest with us, I don't think you intend to make a career in the shoe trade."

Hannah confessed.

"Then I'm afraid you'll have to go, and give someone else the opportunity."

Having been ejected from three places in even fewer months, Hannah decided to take a more positive approach to life. She went home at lunchtime and packed her suitcase while they were downstairs in the shop. Time, she thought, to be somewhere else. She was in trouble again, and she couldn't begin to imagine what more trouble would be like; or how many sackings there would have to be until she came to that black, unfathomable place that was designated by everyone (her father, stepmother, Nicholas, her mother and herself) as "where Hannah would end up." She decided to short-circuit the whole process. She sat on the train heading for Bournemouth and her mother without any strong sense that she was making a final move. But sometimes it's easier to leave before being asked.

*I'd sacrifice anything come what might*
*For the sake of having you near*
*In spite of the warning voice that comes in the night*
*And repeats and repeats in my ear*
*Don't you know little fool*
*You never can win*

*Use your mentality*
*Wake up to reality*
*But each time I do just the thought of you*
*Makes me stop before I begin*
*'Cos I've got you under my skin*

The staff watched the dancing, although not merely with approval. They kept a careful eye on Terry during the Social. And while his movements were smooth and assured as he partnered Hannah around the room to Frank's crooning, he was careful always to keep a good six inches between them. Terry, she had been told, in confidential whispers, was there by Order of the Court. He had a history of sexually assaulting minors, but the judge had given him the chance to have treatment instead of putting him in prison.

"But they watch him all the time. One false move, and he's behind bars," Pat, a fellow patient, told Hannah with a proper sense of drama. "Don't tell anyone about it because it's a secret. No one's supposed to know, to give him a chance to have normalised relationships."

Hannah had become used to the peculiar mix of psychosocial jargon and colloquial speech in which most of the longer-term patients spoke. They prided themselves on having a technical knowledge of their own and other patients' conditions.

In fact, Hannah heard about Terry from half a dozen patients, all of them insisting that she must never mention it to anyone else. Only Terry, and his current girlfriend, Sally, another patient, never spoke about why he was there, which was in itself suspicious, because there was nothing the inmates liked more than describing their illnesses to each other.

Hannah had never come across a sex offender before, and

Terry didn't fit her picture of how people who did that kind of thing should look. Deep down, she didn't really believe it. He was a handsome, well-dressed man in his late twenties, who spoke with a public-school accent. He was always polite and well mannered, and was very attentive to Sally, who seemed flattered to have such an elegant boyfriend. But it was a fact that he wasn't allowed to go out of the hospital grounds, and Hannah noticed whenever she was alone with him in the dayroom, within seconds a nurse would appear from nowhere, and stand or sit nearby until someone else arrived.

Hannah had learned a great deal about people during her four months at the hospital: strange things, the kind of things you don't learn anywhere else. But, surprisingly quickly, even the oddest details of people's lives and problems came to seem almost normal and everyday.

There was Pam, so tall and thin she could have been a model. Pam was twenty-three, and hadn't been outside, except in an ambulance, for five years. She was agoraphobic, Hannah learned. But that wasn't all. She was also claustrophobic and frightened of new people, though no one seemed to know the name of that particular ailment, and she was given to fits of panic for no apparent reason at all. Once, when Pam tried on Hannah's drainpipes, she had a claustrophobic attack because of the tightness of the jeans around her waist and legs, and they'd had to hold her down, writhing and screaming blue murder on the floor, while a nurse cut them off her with a pair of scissors. By then, this was no more than part of an ordinary day for Hannah, and it hadn't really been necessary for the nurse to ask if she was upset by the commotion.

Sally, Terry's girlfriend, had a chronic inferiority complex, according to Pat, who had been in the hospital for two years and was the most adept at jargon. Sally was one of a pair of identical twins: the very twins who a few years before had been on television every night for months advertising home perms. She was the "twin who didn't have the Terri." Or maybe she was the one who did. Pat couldn't remember. But she was certain it was *very* significant that Sally was going out with Terry.

"*Terri*, you see?" Pat explained with a knowing nod. Hannah nodded back. She thought she could see that it was significant, but she was not experienced enough yet in these things to know how, exactly. Every Saturday Sally's twin, Jackie, would come to visit. They really *did* have the same hairstyle, short and waved, and astonishingly, Jackie always arrived wearing exactly the same clothes Sally had on that day. Sally insisted it was because they were psychic with each other, but Hannah noticed after a few weeks that Sally was called to the phone regularly every Friday night. One week, she crept down the stairs to listen and overheard Sally whispering into the mouthpiece.

". . . the pink shirtwaister and black winklepickers."

Hannah was sorry because she liked the idea of telepathic twins. But the harmony between Sally and Jackie didn't go beyond the sartorial.

In the dayroom, Jackie would begin each visit by recounting her week for Sally. There were dances and films and an unending rollcall of boyfriends. Sally sat listening to all this with an increasingly grim face until Jackie had finished and asked, "So what have you been up to?"

Sally, of course, being a patient in a mental hospital, hadn't been up to much. She would offer whatever hospital drama had occurred and talk about Terry and how well they were getting on, and their plans for marriage, later, when he'd finished . . . that is, when they were discharged. Jackie's look of smug satisfaction at the course of her own life turned to distaste as Sally told her about the life of the hospital. It was, her downturned mouth silently said, *not nice*; not a nice thing to talk about. And when Sally got on to Terry, Jackie contrived to look very superior and knowing: a look which clearly had a history in their lifelong relationship and which elicited an automatic response from Sally. Three visits out of four, Sally would stop talking, take a long look at Jackie's expression, and, without any further warning, fly at her twin sister, grabbing handfuls of Terri-waved hair and slapping her carefully made-up face. Usually a nurse was nearby, ready to pull them apart, and Jackie would straighten her clothes with a prissy, self-righteous movement, and leave, telling the nurse that her sister was never going to get better, she had always been like that, mean and envious, and always would be.

Hannah decided it must have been Sally, after all, who didn't have the Terri.

The visits were allowed to continue because the doctors apparently felt Sally had to work through her identity problems. But eventually they were stopped when, one Saturday afternoon, Jackie was found smooching in a dark corner of the entrance hall with Terry, after she'd said goodbye to Sally in the dayroom. Terry swore Jackie had pretended to be Sally, and eventually Sally accepted his version, but she refused to see her sister after that, and it was agreed by her doctor that the visits had better be suspended for the time being.

Douglas never danced. He was as quiet as Danny the MC was boisterous, but he attended all the Socials and watched from his chair with a benign, myopic smile. He was a Scot of indeterminate age, but it was certain that he was younger than he looked. Mild was the essence of Douglas, who was shy to the point of anguish, but eventually managed to have a quiet courteous relationship with most of the patients. People were inclined to tell him their troubles, because he was capable of sitting still for ages and never interrupted beyond a murmured "Oh, dear," or "That's a shame." He wore a tweed jacket that might have belonged to his father and cavalry twill trousers with heavy patterned brown brogues, and walked slowly, which Pat said was as much to do with the heavy tranquillisers he was on, as his natural slowness of temperament.

Pat also related the story about Douglas' only attempt to join the occupational therapy group. He did a painting of a sporran, very carefully, extremely detailed, a bit of a work of art. He was proud enough of it to show it to Pat, and then to his doctor at his weekly session. The reason why Douglas had never returned to occupational therapy was because Dr. Watt (something of a laughable figure among the patients, and, as it happened, a Scot himself) had taken a long moment to consider the painting, and then asked, "And what exactly is this, Douglas?"

"A sporran, Dr. Watt," Douglas explained politely, a little hurt that it wasn't obvious.

"Yes, Douglas, a sporran," the doctor mused, rolling his r's. "And what is behind a sporran?"

Douglas flushed bright red, as he was inclined to do when anything *biological* was mentioned. He was, Pat confided, almost certainly a virgin.

"A kilt," Douglas said, somewhat resourcefully for him.

"That is true," Dr. Watt conceded, a little tetchily. "And what is concealed by the part of the kilt—a *skirt*, mind you—that is hidden by the sporran, Douglas?" he asked, and went on without waiting for his patient to come up with a further obfuscation. "A *weapon*! Am I not right?" He made use of the subliminal pause before answering his own question. "A weapon, Douglas, that is what. A weapon is concealed behind this object you have drawn. You are very angry, aren't you?"

"No," Douglas muttered deep into his chest, and became

thereafter, according to Pat, an even milder version of himself, and an ex-artist.

Hannah never quite worked out what, exactly, was wrong with Pat. She was a skinny, shapeless and spinsterish young woman who wore glasses with lenses half an inch thick, and spoke in a high-pitched, whining voice. Pat gave as full an account of her troubles as she did of others'. She was a depressive, she said, and her problem stemmed from having a neurotic invalid mother whom she had had to look after for most of her thirty odd years. She had never married, hardly had any boyfriends, because her life revolved around the demands of the sick woman. One day, for no particular reason she could recall, after two decades of uncomplaining service, Pat started screaming in the middle of preparing a poultice for her mother's troubled chest. She flung the boiling muddy muck at the old woman, who managed to duck so that the nasty stuff made an unpleasant mess on the wall. After that Pat went very quiet and sat in the corner of the bedroom she had inhabited since childhood, waiting, it seemed, for something to happen. When they came to take her away, she was as relieved as her ailing mother, who was fixed up with a home help, which, frankly, turned out to be a much more satisfactory arrangement for all concerned. Pat had been in the small psychiatric hospital in Bournemouth ever since. On the whole she seemed happy enough, but from time to time she was subject to terrible depressions, when she turned her face to the wall and stared at a fixed point for several days on end. Luckily, some patient-drama always came along that was interesting enough to pull Pat back from her dark place and allow her to take up her role as hospital reporter.

Hannah understood very well when Pat told her about sitting in her room waiting for something to happen. It was what

Hannah had been doing for the past four months. She might, currently, be moving around the dayroom, propelled by the pressure from Terry's body, but her life, and consequently her mind, were static.

She was marking time, and during her first few weeks at the hospital she had learned that there was nothing to be thought about the future. Just as being pushed backwards around the dayroom had no implication for travelling, so the daily activities of sleeping, eating and talking to people were without meaning beyond the moment.

It was a curious condition for a fifteen-year-old to be in. All young children live with part of their minds constantly busy rehearsing the future. The "what happens next" of stories becomes a pattern for their own lives. "When I'm five, I'll be going to school." "When I'm grown up, I'm going to be . . ." "When I get married . . ." And the curiosity about what will be becomes a propellant. At fifteen, a person might be confused by the many but invisible possibilities ahead of her, but very few live without possibilities at all. It would be alien to the restless energy of young human creatures.

But Hannah had run out of possibilities. It was as if the door to the dayroom had vanished and there was nothing beyond circling in strict tempo. She might have panicked, but it seemed she had used up all her panic when she swallowed the sleeping pills her mother kept in the drawer, so she held still, marking time in strictempo, as if waiting for something to happen. But she had not the slightest notion of what it might be. Or rather, she knew there was nothing that *could* happen. So, at fifteen, in the year the Beatles recorded "Love Me Do," she danced her old-fashioned dance and closed down the part of her mind that wrestled with the future.

This was not the reason why she was in hospital. It was not

a sign of Hannah's neurosis. Her sense of the absence of any possible future was fully endorsed by her doctor, the same Dr. Watt who had stifled Douglas' creative impulse. But, in Hannah's case, Dr. Watt was being no more than realistic. And so was Hannah.

There *was* nothing that could happen. Hannah's life was on hold. Dr. Watt, to give him credit, had tried to push it in a direction, to get her father to understand that, in spite of her expulsion, she had to be allowed to go back to school; but having failed, there was little he could do but wait and see. It was generally agreed by the staff that this was the best thing to do, but it was also recognised that it was not possible to keep a child in hospital forever. Eventually, something had to be done, though no one, so far, had come up with any practical solution.

The staff at the Lady Mary Hospital did not consider Hannah to be in need of hospitalisation. That is to say, they did not feel she needed treatment because, although she had arrived after a small overdose and clearly had depressive tendencies, both her act of swallowing the handful of pills, and her depression, were perfectly rational responses to her circumstances. She was not technically mentally ill, but very troubled, and with cause.

She had been admitted to Lady Mary's not on the recommendation of any doctor, but at the insistence of her mother, after Bournemouth General had assured her that Hannah was all right and could be sent home the morning following the pill-swallowing episode. She had demanded her daughter be sent to a psychiatric institution with such vehemence, not to say hysteria, that the admission doctor thought it a good idea to do it to keep Hannah out of her way for a bit, and to give them a chance to find out why the girl had tried to kill herself only two days after leaving her father and moving in with her mother.

They contacted Hannah's father, and the following day he arrived, unhappily at the same time as her mother came to visit. The nurse on duty heard screams in the admission ward and found father and mother standing on either side of Hannah's bed, each turned towards her, their heads almost touching over Hannah's body like the apex of a triangle, shouting at her in unison.

"How dare you do this to me!"

". . . do this to me! You've never been anything but trouble! I'm sick to death of you . . ."

". . . sick to death of you . . . and the trouble you've caused me . . ."

". . . you've caused me . . ."

It was Hannah, in the bed with the covers over her head, who was screaming.

The nurse hustled both adults out of the ward before the rest of the patients began screaming, too. In the office, deprived of the focus of their rage, they began yelling accusations at each other. She blamed him, he blamed her, for this turn of events, their voices rising until their present situation was left behind and pure hatred rang around the corridors of the hospital. Several male nurses and a couple of doctors came running at the commotion, tranquillising injections at the ready, only to discover it was visitors, not patients, they had to separate.

Later, Hannah told Pat that it was the first time in five years her parents had been in the same room, and certainly, when they were standing over her bed, the first time in a great deal longer that they'd agreed about anything.

It was decided that Hannah had better not go back to her father either, for the time being, and since there were no other relatives, the hospital was the only place she could be.

They didn't give her any treatment, apart from a couple of

tranquillisers after her parents' visit. She was not on any drugs, and her weekly sessions with Dr. Watt were brief enough.

"How have things been this week?" he'd ask her.

"Fine, thank you," Hannah would reply.

"Is there anything you want to talk to me about?"

"No, not really."

Then, after a long pause, while they both listened to the silence, Dr. Watt would make ready to get up from his chair.

"Well, if you're sure there's nothing . . ."

Hannah would get up and say goodbye.

Every session was the same. At first, Dr. Watt's "Is there anything you want to talk to me about?" sounded more meaningful to Hannah than was intended. He was a doctor, after all, and all the other patients had their problems aired in their therapeutic sessions. Hannah felt his words were probing for something that he had knowledge of. She started to feel he knew something and was inviting her to tell him about it. But she couldn't think what it might be. Nothing was happening in her life, and she didn't mind that, and therefore there *was* nothing she wanted to say. Yet, perhaps, there was something she couldn't think of, or needed to discuss. She pondered the problem and finally came up with the notion that she was pregnant, and Dr. Watt knew it, but she didn't. She got increasingly alarmed by this phantom pregnancy, in spite of the fact that she had only had one sexual experience, and that two years before, and penetration hadn't occurred. But it is remarkably easy for a troubled young girl to imagine impossible things, particularly when the life of the mind is blank. Eventually, she summoned up courage and responded to Dr. Watt's invariable question, which was, in reality, no more than a concealed way of saying he hadn't come up with any solution to her situation.

"Am I pregnant?"

"I don't know. Are you?" he asked, a little startled at the sudden possibility of Hannah having a future, after all.

"I don't see how I could be, but I thought you might think I was."

She explained about the sexual encounter two years before, and Dr. Watt assured her that she couldn't be pregnant, but that he'd arrange to have her tested to put her mind at rest. After that the future receded once again, they reverted to their regular catechism and Hannah stopped worrying that there might be an answer to his question.

Hannah had soon become accepted as the baby of the Bin. Pat, especially, took her under her wing, but the other patients too looked out for her. If someone got wildly out of hand, throwing things, or themselves, violently about while Hannah was in the room, another patient would tell them to pull themselves together.

"Not in front of Hannah," they'd say. And unless the situation was completely out of control, her presence usually had some calming effect.

Word got back to her old school that Hannah was in terrible circumstances, scrubbing floors in the workhouse or madhouse, depending who was telling the tale; but the truth was that life at Lady Mary's was much more interesting than most places a fifteen-year-old might find herself, and, at the same time, rather safer, calmer even, than she was used to. Apart from the fact that she didn't know how she was ever going to leave, she was not unhappy or frightened in the converted Victorian mansion just up the road from the seafront. She had certainly been both frightened and unhappy for enough of her life before that to know that what she had was asylum in the old, true, sense of the word: a refuge, a breathing space, a place of safety. If this was the place in which everyone said Hannah "would end up" it was by no means the worst she could imagine. Being stuck was not unpleasant, it was downright restful so far as she was concerned. And however much the doctors and nurses might cluck at each other about her continuing presence there, Hannah didn't mind being in the Bin at all. All she had to do was dance an old-fashioned dance round and round the dayroom.

# Shit and Gold

For the purposes of the story, I never had a name. I was always just the daughter of a miller, and then later the Queen—meaning Mrs. King. But we millers' daughters have names, like everyone else, though the archetype-makers would have you think differently, even in a story such as this, where naming names is the name of the game.

Well, I bloody well had a name and have one still—excuse the language, not suited to a queen, I know, but once a miller's daughter, always a fucking miller's daughter, I say. My name, I can reveal, was, and still is, Claraminda Griselda. The first confabulation of a name being an indication of the florid hopes my father had for his own flesh and blood to raise him up above his natural station in life (a hope rather surprisingly granted now that he's been elevated, as the father of a queen must be, to an earldom); the second name my father once heard in a tale told in the local inn by some accountant fellow called Chaser, or Chooser, or Chancer, or something, who fancied himself as more than just an ordinary customs and excise man. My father, the recently elevated earl, told me he had liked the sound of Griselda, and that the story the taxman told had held out great promise for the bearer of that name, who, though she had her troubles, came out well settled in the end.

However, not wishing to antagonise the rest of the village children (my father had already alienated us from our neighbours, on account of his comical fantasies and high-falutin ways), I called myself the rather simpler Clary, and even now, though the King has all the pretensions of a miller and insists on having my full name on documents of state, I think of myself as plain Queen Clary.

I spent my childhood in a miasma of flour dust. No matter how my mother wiped and washed while she lived, it was always possible to write my name with my finger in the film on every surface. Naturally, or rather, unnaturally, my father insisted I went to the village school to learn to read. So while most of my contemporaries were productive elements of their household—carrying water, carding wool, pumping bellows—I sat in school, alone, except for the children of better families than ours, who would not talk to a mere miller's daughter, learning my letters, and what to do with them. I could not see what such an excess of learning would achieve, apart from being able to write my name on stools and tables and windowsills.

Of course, the price of his flour reflected the extraordinary expense my father had in the raising of a mere daughter, so we weren't very popular on that account, either. There were plenty of people who passed through our village with tales of the cost of a sack of flour just a few miles away. I say a few miles, but each one of them might have been a continent for most of the villagers with their broken-down nags and rickety carts. Even then, they would only complete the journey if fortune smiled on them and the brigands kept away. It goes to show—me saying *a few* miles—the way you get used to a new station in life. What would a dozen miles be to me, with all the resources of the stables and a choice of exquisitely crafted carriages at my disposal? If I ever used them, that is. As for brigands: I should be so lucky.

So I grew up in a flour-pale house where even our eyelashes were dusted with pulverised wheat and rye, and learned, in readiness for the future in my pompous father's head, to read. Even now, in my mind's ear, I can hear his bellowing baritone carrying through the air from the mill beside our cottage.

*I care for nobody*
*No, not I—*
*And nobody cares for me.*

They were the truest words that ever came from a man's lips.

So we weren't a very popular little family, and I spent a good deal of time on my own. Often, I'd sit in a corner watching my father at work. Not from any admiration of him, but with fascination at the process he carried out. The two great granite grinding stones were turned by two pairs of donkeys at opposite sides of the stones, going round and round very slowly as if once they had tried to catch each other up, but had finally tired out, and realising they never would manage it, had slowed forever down to a dull and hopeless plod. Actually, there was a series of donkeys—they didn't last long, my father being mean with feed and generous with their work hours. I never cared for them much, they seemed so depressed. What interested me was the process they set and kept in motion.

My father tipped grain into the hopper and it trickled down, like the sand in the hourglass in my husband, the King's, counting house, between the great stones which turned, thanks to the will-less motion of the donkeys, and crushed the grain into a gritty powder. I think it was the relentlessness of the process which fascinated me. Round and round, and on and on. Grain in at the top, flour out at the bottom. An endless process for the endless need of the village for bread. Those grinding stones were at the secret heart of all our lives. Whether they liked it or not, the villagers had need of my father and his mill. No one could manage without bread, and those who had fallen on bad times were obliged to go cap in hand to my father and ask for time to pay for the sacks of flour they could not do without.

He always obliged, but not very obligingly. There are two ways of having people in your debt. You can make it easy, taking the long view that everyone has times of difficulty, but also other times which are not so hard. You treat your debtors as if they were yourself at a different stage of fortune, so that they know when better times come they can take an extra chicken or whatever, and you will rejoice with them in their improved fortune. And there is the other way—my father's way. Everyone in the village owed him at one time or another, and he never let them forget it. He would mark the names of those who couldn't pay him on a slate, with exaggerated care, listening with relish to the screech it made. Other people's hard luck made him feel richer, not just in what they owed him, but in some more mysterious way, as if every degree by which someone else was down pushed him up in his own esteem. "They can't do without me," he would say, booming with self-satisfaction. Then he'd burst into the old chorus:

*I care for nobody*
*No, not I—*
*And nobody cares for me.*

It was a song of triumph. And although the last line was as true as true could be, it didn't worry him. It made him feel bigger and more important in some twisted way to know that nobody, including his daughter, *did* care for him.

I never had much time for my father, and my mother, for the handful of years I knew her, was too preoccupied with drudgery and not getting on the wrong side of him to make much impact on me beyond pity for her lot. She died very quietly, apparently of nothing more than a lack of will to live. Which was probably the truth. She faded away, as if each day proved that there was little and increasingly less to live for.

So I was a solitary child. I watched the stones grinding and listened to the rhythm they made as the slight hollows and bumps in the granite altered the pitch. *Strraagga graast, scrummm, scrummm. Straagga grasst, scrummm scrummm.* It inhabited my dreams, that beat, becoming as much a part of me as my own heart's rhythm. And I was content in spite of my loveless surroundings. Somehow, the perpetual circling of the stones seemed to me very like the shape and movement of the world itself. The village, bread, work, children, seemed to have a pattern, which I knew, for all the ups and downs of fortune, to be a good, solid, pattern. I felt a rightness about how things were, about all the circles that were drawn by each family and each village with the millstones grinding out the rhythm of being alive. And my father, for all his foolish pomposity and grandiose notions, could not help but provide the certainty as he ground the grain around which life made its circles.

Only once, while I was growing up, did the circle pattern fail. A blight on the crops, who knew why, one year, and for a while the grinding stones were silenced. There was no grain to mill, and it was as if my own heart had halted, the silence was so ominous. It was, that time, a localised problem, however, and soon enough grain was brought in from the outside world, and the stones began their *strraagga graast, scrummm scrummm* once again. It was a warning to me, though. That pattern, so close to life itself, was not immutable. The vital circles could be halted. It was a useful lesson to learn.

Of course, the King was nowhere to be seen during that time of hardship. It was not his way to go abroad among his people unless he was certain of their loyalty and affection. And no one in the village doubted that the King had enough grain stored away to get him through difficult times. However, once the millstones were doing their work, he passed through our village in a grand triumphant ride, as if the return of the stuff of life was his doing. People lifted their heads as he passed, magnificent on his great white horse weighted down with plumes and tapestries. They bobbed a curtsey or bowed their heads briefly, while he nodded graciously at them. No one took much notice. The King was not part of the village life, except inasmuch as he taxed and tithed us. No one hated him, he was too remote, too irrelevant for that. They simply saw him as a fabulous creature passing through their byways.

Except my father, of course. He bowed and scraped so much that the King thought him his finest subject. He dismounted and demanded to be taken on a tour of his miller's mill. Oh, my father obliged, with such obsequiousness that I thought I might vomit. I suppose the honour was too much for his miserable mind. At any rate, that is some kind of explanation for what happened next. Faced with the condescending attention of his liege lord, my father entirely lost his head. It was never altogether true that he cared for *nobody*. For the rich and powerful he cared, it seemed, beyond his own sanity and the wellbeing of us both.

My father called me to him, hissing out of the corner of his mouth, while blathering to His Majesty who was about to remount and get on his way back to the relative warmth and comfort of his castle.

"Sire! Sire!" he said, bowing and scraping while from the other side of his smiling face he summoned me. "Where are you, girl? Come here! Come *here*! Sire, may I introduce you . . . she's just coming . . . here in a moment . . . to, yes, here she is . . . (straighten your dress, girl) . . . my daughter, Your Majesty. My daughter, Claraminda Griselda."

My father held me in front of him by my shoulders, his fingers digging into my flesh in his excitement. The King looked at me and smiled a vague, royal smile. Frankly, I wasn't the prettiest girl a king had ever laid eyes on. Not *ugly* you understand, but nothing really special. He was again about to turn and go when my agitated father, seeing no light in His Majesty's eyes, let out a strangulated sound, a screech not unlike the sound of a debtor's name being marked on the slate.

"Your *Majesty*!"

And the King turned at the urgency of his cry. My father now had to think up the rest of the sentence. But "thinking" isn't a good description of what he did.

"Your Majesty, this is no ordinary girl. No mere miller's daughter, Sire. No, she is a remarkable child. Not just dutiful and clever, though she is that, of course, but something more, much much more . . ."

We all waited to see how my father would complete his babblings. I supposed madness mixed with insatiable greed came to the rescue.

"This child, this young woman, Your Majesty . . . has an extraordinary gift . . . given to no one else. You see, Sire, she can . . . she has the ability . . . gained from God himself, it must have been . . . she can . . . spin . . . straw into . . . gold."

There was an astonished silence while my father stared at the King, his eyes bugging almost out of his head as he himself heard the preposterous thing he had said. Everyone else looked at him: the King, myself, the whole retinue. I thought for a moment that the King was going to have my father arrested for ridiculousness, but when I dragged my eyes away from my demented creator and took in His Majesty, I saw his expression change from disbelief at what he was hearing to something very like my father's when someone came to him to put themselves deeply in his debt. I saw the King's eyes glaze over with lust at the idea of monstrous wealth and power.

"Your Majesty . . ." I said, trying to think of something to excuse my father and prevent him from being thrown into the country's deepest, blackest dungeon for the rest of his life. I did not love my father, but still I felt that the blood between us was enough to make me want to try and salvage his life.

"Be quiet, girl!" my father shouted, though he needn't have bothered; I couldn't think of a thing to say that might mitigate the nonsense he had spoken.

His Majesty turned his head to me, and the former complete lack of interest in the plain miller's daughter was transformed, as if my fairy godmother had waved a wand and made me the most exquisite maiden in the land. I immediately understood my position, and a shiver of despair ran through me. I was locked between the gaze of two avaricious men, each of whom saw me as the means vastly to improve his own standing. What hope had I, imprisoned between the hungry stares of father and king? It was as if a sentence of death had already been pronounced on me, before His Majesty ever said a word.

"Is that so, miller?" the King finally said, never taking his eyes off me for a second. "Straw into gold, you say?"

A look of fear crossed my father's face, as for the first time he realised what would happen to him (never mind me, of course) when his ludicrous boast was proved to be a lie.

"Your Maj . . ." he began, but what could he say to retrieve the situation? The words had flown from his mouth and nothing would make them unsaid.

Funnily enough, the King did not think to ask me about my unusual skill. Nobody thought to say anything to me at all. You could see the King wavering between his eagerness for such a thing to be true—because if so, he would be the beneficiary of a treasure beyond the dreams even of kings—and the thought that he was being made a fool of. There was nothing he liked less than people trying to make a fool of him; just the idea put him into an executionary frame of mind. You could see his weighing up the benefits and the risks of believing my father. You might say that my father's story was so preposterous that no one could give a second's credence to what he said. But that would be to underestimate the power of greed. Our future, my father's and mine, hung in the balance, as the seconds passed. Our very lives depended on the King being as avid a greedy fool as my father. It was all we could hope for.

The King stared dangerously at my father when he spoke again.

"Well, let us see, miller, what wonders this daughter of yours can perform. I will take her to my castle, and if she can indeed turn straw into gold, then I will marry her. If not, the pair of you will die so that the world can see I am not a monarch to be fooled with."

Now, it has probably crossed your mind that it's a damn strange thing for a girl to become a wife purely on the grounds of being able to spin straw into gold. She could become your banker, yes, but why a wife? Of course, it has to do with the needs of the structure within which we were all of us imprisoned—the story. That's how it goes in this corner of the narrative world: the prize for doing the impossible is to become the wife of a king. Nothing to be done about that. Not even the fact that I cherished the idea of this particular king for my husband as much as I cherished the idea of my father being my father. But we have no choice, characters such as we. Nor could I, given my lack of regard for His Majesty, decide to sit in his palace and flatly refuse to change his straw into gold (if I could have done so, which common sense would tell you I couldn't), preferring to die than live out a miserable life as queen. Like the circular life of the village, I was caught up in a pattern, though this pattern was a great deal less to my liking than the everyday life of the world I inhabited.

My father threw a desperate look at me as I rode away, perched on the back of some flunkey's horse, as if begging me not to let him down now that his life depended on me. Brilliant! All I had to do to keep us both alive was spin straw into gold. Why hadn't he made up something *really* difficult for me to accomplish? In fact, it seemed to me that straw into gold might be relatively easy: I only had to join the ranks of magicians and alchemists and tinker with potions of this and that, and perhaps, given a lifetime of esoteric study and all the luck in this world and the next, come up with the philosopher's stone to realise my father's boast and achieve the King's dreams. The real problem facing me, however, was a great deal more fundamental: I didn't know one end of a spinning wheel from another. I'd been far too busy being prepared at school for my social climbing to learn anything useful like how to spin. I was, quite frankly, absolutely useless with my hands.

I was installed in an out-of-the-way room in the castle. Up everlasting winding stairs, to a room at the top of a turret. Since it was circular, it had commanding views of the whole area. I suppose looking down on the world I had previously been a part of was what my father had intended for me, but, quite honestly, I had other things on my mind than the view.

Half the room, a semi-circle as it were, was filled with a great mound of straw; the other half was empty except for a spinning wheel, and me standing staring at it. The deal was, I spin all the straw into gold by morning, or else. Some deal. Also I knew my way around stories of this kind, being of them as well as in them. I knew as well as anyone about the rule of three. Once never does in this kind of tale, and I was certain that I'd have to perform my miracle times three. Frankly, it didn't matter this time, since I couldn't do what I had to do, anyway. But in general, it's a most dispiriting law. Knowing you have to do everything three times takes the sense of achievement away before you've even started. One might be thrilled to have done something brave, or clever, or impossible the first time, but knowing you have to do it twice more takes immediate gratification away. Even having three wishes loses its charm. You can be sure you'll get one of them wrong and lose the benefit of the other two.

However, that was all rather theoretical as I stood in the turret room staring at the spinning wheel without the faintest idea how it worked. I grant you, it was an interesting piece of psychology, worrying about not knowing how the spinning wheel worked, as though if I'd known everything would be all right. But if you're going to die, you have to pinpoint a single, simple reason. The fact that I didn't know how to turn straw into gold seemed an absurd reason for dying, so I transferred it all on to the spinning wheel. It seemed more acceptable somehow to die because I didn't know how to do the simplest, rather than the most difficult, thing.

The question I held in my mind was: did I really mind about dying and leaving a world where fathers and kings (and, it ought to be said, ineffectual mothers) caused one to be in such a predicament? Put that way, my fate seemed less unacceptable. Still, I was young, barely fourteen, and I had not used up all my optimism about what might lie ahead for me. So, quite honestly, I was not quite reconciled to my forthcoming fate.

I perched on the wooden stool attached to the spinning wheel and identified a sticking-up thing in front of me as a spindle. That's education for you. What I was supposed to do with it, I had no idea, but I knew it by name. I pushed the wheel around listlessly listening to its wobble and creak with growing interest. It had in some way a relationship to the pattern of sound made by my father's grinding stones. Not surprising really, both being circular and designed to go round and round. The rhythm was a comfort to me. By morning, and the end of my life, I thought, I'd be quite consoled.

I can't say how long I'd been doing that when I heard a gratingly high-pitched voice coming from behind me.

"Quite a pickle you're in, isn't it?"

And there, of course, was a skinny little man with a most unpleasant leer on his wrinkled, disagreeable face. Well, I don't need to tell you that he said he could help me, but that there would be a price. My ring, I said. All right, he said. And he set to work.

But knowledge is a terrible thing. How could I be delighted

with my magical escape when I knew that tomorrow the same scenario would occur, and that the night after that I would have run out of ornaments to barter with? Yes, yes, I thought, so the room is filled with gold where there had been straw, but was I really any better off? At best I would become the Queen of this King, and what kind of compensation would that be for my suffering and anxiety? Riches, power even, if I played my cards right. Nice frocks, and servants to take care of them, but I had an intuition that all those things would pall before long, and when they did I would *still* be married to a pig of a man whom I disliked almost as much as my father.

On the third night, in the unwavering way these stories have, I'd promised the firstborn of my marriage. Things will sort themselves out, I thought, in the way things do. And I concluded it was, on balance, better to be alive than dead. More opportunity.

And then the marriage announcement, the wedding, the raising of my father to his earldom, the wedding night. Each of those events, and in particular the latter, filled me with disgust. Best leave it at that. Suffice it to say that kings do not necessarily carry their royalty into the bedroom. Once the fur and finery were off I might as well have been at it with the local shepherd boy. As a matter of fact, having been at it with the local shepherd boy for several months before my new life began, I can tell you I missed him that night—and for a good few thereafter.

That shepherd boy was no slouch in the carnal knowledge and skills of love department, and he taught me a thing or two, but His Majesty had such a depressing effect on me I could not bring myself to practise any of the interesting tricks I had learned. Eventually, my Lord and Master tired of ploughing into me while I lay there limp, with nothing more than my fists clenched, and went on to entertain himself with some of the likelier lasses from the village (all of whom, it must be said, had also learned everything they knew from that delightful young shepherd—how he had learned these things, I wouldn't like to say, but I wager the sheep could tell a tale or two if they had the power of speech).

Nine months later, as sure as fairy tales are fairy tales, I gave birth to a young son, heir to the throne. Huge celebrations, and the return of the wizened little man. Now, I wasn't all that attached to my offspring. Frankly, I would have given him away—I hardly ever saw him in any case, he was nannied and wet-nursed and kept in isolated splendour in the nursery wing of the castle. But I didn't fancy explaining to the King that I'd swapped his son for a load of old straw, even though he would have had only his own greed to blame for it.

"Very well, then," said the little old man, predictably. "I will give you a chance. If you can guess my name within three . . ."

"Oh, please," I interrupted. "Don't you get tired of this nonsense? 'Guess my name. Three days.' And what would you want with a baby, anyway? Listen, I have an alternative suggestion."

The wizened little man was not pleased to have been stopped in mid cliché. He stood staring at me open-mouthed, and was, I'm sure, about to ignore what I said altogether and simply carry on with his pre-programmed deal. I daresay he was unable to consider even the possibility of an alternative. I carried on before he could.

"I've got a better idea. More interesting for both of us. Why don't you give me three days to make *you forget* your name?"

He was flabbergasted, and screwed up his face in confusion, trying to think out this new angle on an old story.

"But . . ." he spluttered eventually. "That's not the way it's done. You have to discover my name. You've got to find it out. Names. It's about names."

"But actually it's not very interesting, is it? All that happens is that I send out my servants who creep about and listen in doorways, and eventually—though, granted, at the last minute—you can be sure one of them will come across you in a wood cackling your name to yourself in premature self-congratulation, and the game will be up. What's clever or amusing about that? A rich and powerful woman uses her servants to find something out. Big deal. Now, what I'm suggesting is another thing altogether. Think of how difficult it is to make a person forget his name. Especially someone with as rare and interesting a name as I'm sure yours must be."

Still bemused, he scratched his head. "How would you do that?"

I smiled at him.

I'd better explain something about myself. Just as I wasn't your archetypal beauty of a miller's daughter, I also did not have the same hankerings after pretty golden princes as my peers were universally supposed to have. Don't ask me why. A matter of personal taste. The King, as handsome as a former fairytale prince must be once he's stopped being a frog, left me cold. I had always been attracted to—how can I put it?—the unusual. The shepherd boy was no one's idea of an Adonis; he suffered badly from the after-effects of chickenpox, and had a body which at best could be called weedy. But once he did the things he did, I came to love each and every pock mark on his pallid cheeks, and lay in my bed at night entertaining myself with visions of his skinny thighs and thin, unmanly, rounded shoulders. It's fascinating how human desire can find all manner of things exciting once it's been given a push in the right direction. Beauty, muscularity, height and thick manes of hair didn't do a thing for me. There it was. Apart from the pock-marked shepherd, I had had another regular liaison with the girl at the dairy—a blowsy, bulbous, ruddy-cheeked creature, bovine like her charges, but as lusty and lewd as any you might hope to meet in a cowshed while collecting the milk in the early dawn. I did not know what to call what the two of us did in the hay together every morning, but I enjoyed it no end, and our frolics added nicely to the detail I was accumulating with my shepherd lad. My tastes were, therefore, catholic, and desire was to me to be found where it may. I did not dismiss the possibility of lascivious, unwedded bliss with someone simply because they did not conform to the current form of beauty dictated by our fairytale existence.

The little man, as stringy as a newborn foal and half my height, with a face so wrinkled that his wrinkles had wrinkles, intrigued me. All that nervous energy, hopping about from one foot to another, his wide thin lips all aquiver, and violent cornflower-blue stark-staring eyes. Everybody has something about them which can be found attractive.

"Come here," I said. "I've got something to show you."

For the statutory three nights he came to my queenly bedroom, and I did indeed show him such things as he'd never even dreamed about. Each morning, at dawn, he'd stagger from my royal room, moaning and murmuring things to himself as if he were trying to lodge impossible truths in his brain. I used and passed on everything I'd learned during my glorious times with the shepherd and the dairymaid, and the scrawny, twisted little man trembled and mewed, night after long, slow night, with the results of my expertise. Each morning, as he limped, his muscles wrenched and ragged, away from my bed, I stopped him and asked him: "Little man, what is your name?"

On the first morning he stopped his muttering and turned achingly towards me on the bed with a wild look in his eye. After a moment of enormous effort, he managed to raise his voice enough so that I could hear what he said.

"My name . . ." he croaked. "My name is . . . Rumpel-Stilts . . ."

And then his eyes went vague as something disappeared into the mist that was his mind. I smiled and said how much I was looking forward to the coming night.

On the second morning, I asked him the same question as he was leaving. Again, he turned, but this time it took much longer to bring the words out into the world.

"My name . . . My name . . . is . . . My name is . . . Rumple . . ."

And he fell silent. I bid him a warm *Good day.*

On the third morning, he was barely able to reach the door, his thin little legs were shaking so much. Great sighs came from him as each foot touched the floor and sent a shuddering memory of bliss and agony shooting through him.

"Little man, what is your name?" I asked him gently.

A strange, almost strangulated sound came from his depths and stuck fast in his throat. His mouth worked and his eyes rolled while he quivered from head to foot, as if every ounce of himself were involved in the effort to think what I could possibly mean by my words. But nothing came.

"What is your name?" I said again.

But the little man had given up, and merely shook his head in wonder and confusion as he disappeared from my room, like a shadow slipping beneath a door.

And so my life is just as my father had dreamed. I am a rich and powerful woman. The Queen of all and everything. I am respected, even revered for my wisdom and carefully-considered decisions. The King, these days, is too busy to attend to matters of state, so I make sure that everything runs well and for the benefit of all the people. My father, the *arriviste* Earl, assists the

King in his never-ending task, so he also doesn't have much time to visit his royal daughter, nor to attend to the mill, and I have placed it in the safe and talented hands of the shepherd boy, who says it makes a nice change from tending sheep. In order to maintain this satisfactory state of affairs, I arrange for the turret room with the spinning wheel (I still have not learned how to use it—just as well, considering the risk and result of pricking one's finger on the spindle, in a world such as ours) to be filled every day with straw-spun gold.

So the King is in his counting house most of the time, these days, along with my father, counting out his money. There's so much to count, I'm afraid they will never get to the end of it. And while they are thus engaged, I run the country, dispensing just law, and keeping the millstones grinding, and all the necessary circles turning. And for entertainment? For entertainment, I have my milk delivered fresh to the castle every morning, and at night I summon my little man from his day's spinning, and, over and over again, make him forget his name.

# Short Circuit

It was Lillian's habit to take a walk every lunchtime. It got her out of the office, she avoided having to eat with the colleagues she already spent most of her week with, and gained a daily dose of fresh air. A nonsense, of course, in an inner-city park with traffic racing and fuming round its perimeter, but the landscaped greenery and docile duck-life in the man-made pond gave at least a symbolic justification for Lillian's feeling that it was good for her. Anyway, it didn't do any harm.

Lillian felt also that her daily walk was good for her mind, though if thinking was a deliberate consideration of particular matters about which one came to a judgement, then that probably wasn't the right word for what went on in her head as she walked the winding path that took her back to where she had started, in just the right amount of time to begin the afternoon's work. Her thought processes didn't seem to function in the deliberate, one-step-after-another way of her daily walks, on their defined route.

This really didn't matter since she was not a professional thinker. She supposed, though she wasn't sure, that philosophers and scientists thought in an orderly, arranged way. First there was a problem, then the pros and cons of a possible solution and finally a decision which might mean the end of that particular thought, or the choosing of a new solution to be mentally tested. Even if this were an accurate picture of that kind of mind—and she wasn't convinced it was—her life didn't require such an orderly approach to thought. She didn't think she thought about anything very much during her lunchtime walks.

At least that was how it had been, until a couple of months ago. But then she reminded herself as she reached the part of the path which looped itself around the oval duck pond, everything had been the way it had been until that time. Since when, her lunchtime walks had lost their pleasantly pointless flavour, her mind seeming blank enough to do no more than notice the recurring influence of the seasons: leaf-fall and the stark silhouettes of naked branches; new growth and the strange, almost hallucinatory suggestion of pale green like the fuzz on the chin of an adolescent boy; male mallards in their bright mating colours; ranks of ducklings struggling to keep up in the race for the bread Lillian threw to them, but which their mothers always seemed to get to first. That had been what the walks were for; just noticing the same things as the years rolled by—now this is happening again, now that. She valued them for the relaxation that repetition offered. Like the path which led, in space, always to the same sequence of landmarks, the changing seasons provided a similar comfort in time. All Lillian did, or wanted to do, was effortlessly to notice. But although it was now palpably winter—her heavy overcoat and scarf, and the slap of cold air against her cheeks telling her it was so—her mind was too preoccupied to benefit from the pleasure of *here it is again*. She wondered, though, if what went on in her mind lately would be counted as "thought," either.

This morning, as she put up with the daily crush on the tube getting to work, a memory of part of a conversation before dinner last night had come into her mind, gleaming and sharp, like a bright, lethal blade.

"I'll be a bit late this evening. I'm having a drink with Rory."

"Who?"

"Rory, from God-knows-when in my life. He phoned out of the blue, this morning."

"How do I know that's true?"

The sentence had slipped out in spite of Lillian trying to hold it in by sinking her teeth into her bottom lip.

"Because," the voice calm, without emotion one way or the other, "because I say so."

End of conversation. Time for a drink before dinner.

On the tube, surrounded by damp, overheated bodies which Lillian would smell on her clothes from time to time during the day, there were two passes from the gleaming, double-edged knife. The memory of having tried and failed—again, always again—to bite back useless words that couldn't possibly resolve the question constantly paining her, made her almost faint with anger at herself. Until she remembered how deliberately he'd said, "*He* phoned me out of the blue . . ." The emphasis on *he* hadn't been there as he spoke, but that was what the sentence was for. Allay suspicion, leave no room for it. Rory. *He*.

The direction of her anger shifted now from her own inability to live with her doubts, to Charlie, for his deceit, his scheming, and for the way his deceit made her feel. The rage at being lied to. The energy it took up.

There were flashes before her eyes as if chemicals surged suddenly in her body, causing a visual disturbance. She saw a picture of Rory—female—telling whoever she was involved with, "I'm seeing Charlie tonight. You remember, the girl I was at college with?" Why not use the coincidence of a pair of cunningly ambiguous names? Make up as little as possible. Always the best way. And then laugh about it together.

Out in the street with enough empty air around her, she shook off the pressure of bodies pushing, close in, against her, and got hold of her thoughts. This had to stop. It was too painful, too awful. Charlie had told her again and again, "Listen to me, I love you. Why else would I be here? What other possible reason could there be for it? Don't you know, don't you feel I love you? Can't you tell?"

Lillian let the familiar assurance spread over her sore parts like a viscous remedy taken to line and soothe raw flesh. There was a simple logic to Charlie's words. Truth was self-evident. Well, that wasn't necessarily true, but in this case it was. She couldn't, if she looked at the history of the two of them, at his behaviour, at how things were between them, doubt that he loved her. And the corollary: "I'm not interested in anyone else. I love you—I want you. You are everything I've ever wanted, why would I go with anyone else?"

It was insane—well, neurotic—to give time and energy to suspicions that made no sense in the light of what was actually happening.

She climbed the flight of stairs to the office, relieved at the calm certainty—as normal as Charlie, as anyone—she had made herself feel. It was the state of mind in which she wanted to proceed with her day and her life.

It had lasted until lunchtime. Her emotional existence had

taken on a new diurnal pattern: the second-thought rage about something said or done as the tube clattered along in time to the build-up of her anger; the coming to her senses as she walked to work, once the pressure of being underground was relieved by being back on the surface again; the simple getting on with her job until lunchtime, when she went downstairs and headed towards the park, and then the other version of "coming to her senses," and an hour of striding rage. A daily nightmare since Charlie had moved in with her. It was unbearable—whether her suspicions were accurate or not—just the thinking, the supposing, the turmoil of one minute this certainty, the next minute the opposite. It reminded her how, as a child, she had believed in God because it was so clear, so obvious, that he existed. She couldn't imagine how anyone could think differently. And then, ten years on, the same absolute conviction that there was no deity, no otherness, only the material world that could be seen, heard and felt. How could anyone possibly believe in God? It wasn't until a further ten years on that she had come to the possibility of agnosticism, and the ability to live with an uncertainty. Even then, she had trouble understanding how anyone could believe firmly one way or the other. But the business of believing in Charlie was more urgent than her problems with God. The swings of conviction—he is seeing someone else—he most certainly isn't—came around several giddying times a day. Sometimes Lillian felt as if she were going mad, but there was nothing mad about her thoughts in either state of mind. They were all too logical. It was only the persistence and the see-sawing that had the quality of madness.

She had told Charlie it wouldn't work. She kept on telling him, but it seemed that they had different definitions of what *working* meant. Lillian was at a loss to know what to do. She didn't understand the situation, had no idea how to assess what was going on, all she knew was the vivid quality of her discomfort.

Lillian had never lived with anyone, not until she was thirty-five and Charlie moved in. Barged in, she would have said, but she had enough respect for the truth to know it couldn't have happened without her consent, without her *wanting* it. Nonetheless, it felt now more as if she had been involved in an accident, than that she had made a considered decision. She couldn't shake off the feeling that an act of God had occurred of which she was the victim.

This was not the truth. Lillian had very definitely made a decision, but looking back on it, it seemed to her that that moment was the root of the madness which had descended on her. It had started there: with a thought-out attempt to be . . . normal?

There had always been lovers. Lillian liked sex, and sometimes liked to have company. After a few years of getting together with men purely for their talent in bed, she came round to the view that there might be something better to be found. She confined herself to relationships, thereafter, with men who were talented in bed, *and* whom she could stand to have in her flat for more than five minutes after they'd got dressed. Lillian saw this as a definite moment of growth. At twenty-six, when she made the decision, she had, she felt, matured. Sex on its own was all right, physically, but would no longer do. She felt she wanted more. So from then on she only got involved with men she liked. This caused a decrease in sexual activity, but she was able to cope with it, given her new-found maturity.

At first, at the beginning of Lillian's sexual history, she was no different from her friends, who had as frequent and superficial relationships as she had. They all had fun, Lillian and her friends, through college. But, gradually, one after another, the other women dropped away as each formed permanent attachments. By the time Lillian was thirty-two, most had married or were living with someone, though some had divorced by then and were on second husbands, and two had decided to be lesbians (which made no difference since both of them were in settled relationships). Only Lillian remained steadfastly single. No one stayed in her flat for more than one night at a time, and her newly discovered dissatisfaction with purely physical relationships did not mean that she felt the need to be with someone twenty-four hours a day, or to have company when she went to the supermarket.

She still saw some of those friends and they frequently tried to persuade her of the joys of being in a committed relationship, but it was not what Lillian wanted. She didn't argue when they called her neurotic, she acknowledged it.

"Yes, I suppose I am, but there it is. Here I am, and neurotic or not, I live and work and function okay. So if I don't have a problem, why not just accept that's how I am?"

Fair enough, but, in fact, Lillian did see a psychotherapist for a while. She went because of car tax. She found keeping her car on the road caused her terrible anxiety. For two months before the road tax was due to be renewed each year, Lillian would be overcome with fear and helplessness. The car needed an MOT, but she was somehow incapable of finding, or getting to, a garage to obtain it. She always did eventually, at the last moment, but until then she would lie awake until it began to get light, consumed with worry about how to find a garage, about making an appointment, then getting to it. All this, night after night, for months before, and then a blind panic a day before the tax was due. Afterwards, always, she wondered what the fuss was about; it had been simple, she only had to repeat next year what she had done this year, but calmly. But, of course, the following year the same thing happened. All kinds of official, required organisation left her in this state, and Lillian knew that there was something wrong about it. It made life a misery and she was aware, with one part of her mind, that it wasn't necessary. She went to see a shrink.

There was, in her fear of coping with everyday details, something of a hankering for a "man about the house." So David Fanshaw suggested, and in all honesty, Lillian found herself unable to protest much at his analysis as far as it went. Very soon, though, she was confronted with the problem of *transference*. She was too guarded, Fanshaw told her. After a few weeks, he pointed out that not once had she made a slip of the tongue, she recalled no dreams, and her refusal to lie on the couch, as opposed to sitting opposite him in the chair, was symptomatic of a refusal to trust him, to be prepared to make herself vulnerable to him. They had long since stopped talking about cars and getting domestic machinery mended. Vulnerability had become the issue.

"But why would I deliberately make myself vulnerable?" she asked, her eyes widening in genuine perplexity.

"Because people who refuse to be vulnerable, who refuse to take a risk with other people, are hampered in their ability to make relationships."

"Are you telling me that to open yourself up to being hurt and unhappy is a sign of health? You aren't really saying that, are you? That I should deliberately lay myself open to pain? Wouldn't your lot call that masochistic? There are some genuinely unpleasant people out there, you know."

David Fanshaw made a church roof and steeple with his fingers.

"Until you take the risk, how do you know what anyone is

like? If you reject everyone, because some people aren't nice, you won't find the other kind. You'll never make a real relationship."

"But," Lillian explained calmly, "I don't want a real relationship. I mean, not more than I have already. I see people. I get involved with people . . ."

"Up to a point."

"Well, of course, up to a point. Everything's up to a point. Why would I change my life when it seems very satisfactory to me? I don't *have* to be married to be happy."

"But you're here."

"Because of panicking about *things*, not because I'm not in a cosy domestic situation."

They carried on for a while, but Lillian never did lie down, and it became clear that David Fanshaw felt they wouldn't get to the bottom of things until she responded in a less rational way.

One problem was that Lillian was not mystified about why she was like she was. She knew that her background, a pair of hopelessly inept, over-anxious parents and an older sister killed in a pointless and awful accident, made her attitude to life the way it was. She told Fanshaw that at the first session.

"I understand why I'm the way I am, but how I am, preferring to live alone and so on, is fine by me. I don't want to be cured of my need for independence, I just want some help with my irrational anxieties."

"I'm afraid that psychotherapy doesn't work like that," he warned her. "It's not a matter of curing inconvenient symptoms, but of looking at underlying causes, at the whole situation."

She should have realised then that there wasn't any point, but she kept on hoping that something useful would come out of it. One night, though, she had what David Fanshaw might have called an insight if it had been the kind of thing he approved of. Lillian got up early, wrote a letter to Fanshaw thanking him for his help and enclosing a final cheque, and then put a small ad in the local newspaper offering her car for sale. *That* was what she called dealing with a problem. She couldn't panic about the car if she didn't have one. She promised herself to deal with other anxieties as they arose, in much the same way. If they cause you trouble, do without them. She was only applying to machinery what she had always applied to men. Get rid of whatever areas she found intolerable. Deny the power of anything that could upset her equilibrium. Practical, was the way Lillian thought about it.

So how did it come about that a year after she'd met Charlie, he'd turned up at her doorstep with his suits over one arm, and his stereo under the other? Because she had agreed that he should. And why, Lillian wondered as if it were an entirely new thought, throwing the crusts of her sandwich at the ducks, had she agreed to such a thing?

Because she loved Charlie; because it was different. And because, recognising the pleasure she got from his company and wanting more of it, more of the time, she had thought why *shouldn't* she take a risk, for once in her life? But if love was what she felt for Charlie, it wasn't the blinding kind that her friends seemed to catch. She wasn't befuddled into believing herself to be part of a fairy tale. She had no doubt that the relationship would end sooner or later, or, at any rate, peter out. She could imagine only too well the unpleasantness of separating the effects of two lives that had come together in one place. She could see with dismal clarity, when she forced herself, the misery of finding herself alone after a year or two, disoriented by the new kind of existence she had got used to; or worse, the hideous near-certainty of becoming the woman who waited at home while her man found himself more interesting fish to fry without wanting the inconvenience of packing his bags.

Knowing all this, certain that all this applied to her and not some statistical other, Lillian had nevertheless taken a deep breath and said, "Yes," when Charlie told her for the tenth time that he wanted to be living with her. After all, it seemed suddenly to occur to her, what was the prospect of pain, however clearly she envisaged it, compared to the excitement of doing what she wanted to do, and, *for once*, to hell with the consequences? Which was a curious thought, since until that moment, she had not felt that the life she chose to lead was anything other than exactly what she wanted.

But throwing caution to the wind is a talent that comes with practice, and Lillian had none. A whim, novel though it might be, wasn't enough to stop the cold sweat that ran down her spine when Charlie rang the doorbell on the day they had arranged he should move in. So Lillian, learning from the motorcar lesson, took things in hand.

"Listen," she said while Charlie filled the space in the wardrobe she had made for him. "I want to get something straight. I want to make a deal. I won't be told lies. In return for you not lying to me, I won't make any demands about fidelity. It's just logical," she said, as Charlie turned to look at her. "If I don't care about you fucking other women, then you *can't* lie to me, can you, because there's nothing to lie about. And then I won't have to spend energy worrying if I'm being lied to. It's the idea of being deceived and not knowing it, not you fucking other women, that I really can't stand."

"You don't care if I have other women?"

"No."

Charlie turned to the wardrobe and started taking out the hangers he had just put in.

"What are you doing?"

"I don't want to live with you if you don't care if I'm fucking other people. I'd rather leave now."

Lillian stared at him. "Stop it."

"No. The arrangement isn't to my taste. I *am* faithful to you, and that's all there is to it. I don't want you not to care if I fuck someone else."

"It's just that I don't want you to have a chance to lie to me. I can't bear the idea of worrying about it."

"I don't lie to you. I won't ever lie to you. I don't want other women, because I want you, but if I did, I'd tell you, because it'd be over."

"How do I know that's true?"

"Because I'm telling you it's true."

It was the first time that pair of sentences were spoken between them, but by no means the last. Lillian recognised the essential truth of the exchange, or rather, recognised that it was as far as truth could go in such matters. She had already solved the problem: if she wanted guarantees about another person's thoughts and acts, then she simply had to distance herself sufficiently from them, so that their thoughts and acts were not relevant, and only the actual time spent together was of concern. But something had made her want more.

Perhaps it was simply the passage of time—being thirty-five makes you notice that time is limited and that it's entirely possible for some things never to happen. It also had to do with what might be thought of as a pull towards democracy. If everyone else was taking risks, shacking up with someone and accepting the consequences, then maybe her fear of it *was* wrong. Maybe she should try it.

Whatever it was, when she was faced with the reality, she

discovered that her fears were not merely "neurotic," as in "superficial," but ran deep enough to take up most of her mental energies. She knew she could never know what was really going on in another person's mind, no matter how closely they might have linked their lives, and Lillian found the inescapable reality of this fact intolerable.

"I want to rummage through the files inside your mind," she had once said to a sleepy Charlie, who had smiled at the idea, not realising the deadly seriousness of the thought.

That fact, combined with what seemed to be her congenital certainty that, after a time, all relationships became at best comfortable, and that men would inevitably look elsewhere for excitement, made living with Charlie a kind of hell, as bad as her worst imaginings.

Lillian couldn't understand friends whose confidence in their men seemed to her like a desperate optimism. It seemed that all of them, for the most part, intelligent, well-informed women, believed at the beginning of their involvements that *their* relationship was the final choice of partner that each party would make. They had found their life-long relationship, and, in spite of both the men and the women having had several other relationships, Lillian's friends were wonderfully sure that this was *it*. Never mind the divorce statistics, never mind the figures showing the percentage of men (and women) who were unfaithful in relationships, never mind the fact that some of their friends' marriages had collapsed into apathy or desertion.

Lillian couldn't understand the "It's different for us" attitude that she saw all around her. She didn't feel like that. She couldn't help knowing that statistics had as good a chance of applying to her as to anyone else. So there was no doubt that Charlie, ardent and devoted as he might be at their relatively early stage of relationship, would end up wanting a comfortable domestic relationship with her (if such a thing were possible), and sexual excitement with a variety of someone elses. No, she didn't really think he was unfaithful to her now (at least, for part of the time she didn't), but she knew he would be, and she was horrified at the idea that there would be a moment when the change occurred and she would be left foolishly imagining that it was still the way it had been at the beginning. "Bastard!" she yelled at the faithless Charlie of the future. "Treacherous, lying bastard!" And sometimes, when she couldn't stop herself, she said it to the Charlie of the here and now. It wasn't that she wept and screamed; their discussions were no more than that. But Lillian knew, for all the apparent reasonableness of her tone, that she couldn't believe what Charlie said, and, most awful, she knew she never would. There was nothing he could say. Her questions and accusations were more like verbal tics. They could not be answered.

"But you'd know if I was involved with someone else," Charlie tried to reassure her, defending his future against her pessimism.

She knew, though, that was just another truism not borne out by the figures.

"But you can't punish me, or throw me out for what I haven't done but might do in the future." Charlie was remarkably patient with what he called "LM," which stood for "Lillian's madness."

Enjoy what there is now, and let the future take care of itself. Lillian heard this advice from everyone. It made very good sense. They were, she and Charlie, amazingly happy together; she *did* enjoy having breakfast with him; she *liked* them going to the supermarket together; she looked forward to getting home and meeting him, as she often did, on the doorstep, each fumbling in their pocket for the key. Against all the odds their relationship was a huge success. Except for those times when Lillian's alarm about what was *going* to happen cut through the pleasure, and made her brain zing with anger at Charlie for bringing potential deceit into her life.

Lillian threw her last piece of bread into the mêlée at the edge of the pond and, seeing no more coming their way, the ducks veered off in search of other lunchtime philanthropists. She didn't view their behaviour as treacherous; it was perfectly natural that they should take what they wanted from wherever they could get it. Lillian liked the openness of the transaction.

Everything about human transactions, on the other hand, was devious, including attempts at openness. All right, so Charlie, loving her and wanting her, assured her that he wasn't sleeping around; but when he grew tired of her, he would use *exactly the same words* to lie with. He would say "No" to her question, "Are you fucking anyone?" *now*, because he wasn't, and *then*, because he was. How could anyone know which was which, or when the one turned into the other?

Lillian continued her walk. The path straightened up and took her past neatly manicured grass. In the summer, it was filled with people sunning themselves singly or in couples, with kids racing and shouting, with balls and bikes, dogs and picnickers; now, it was empty, a quiet, green swathe, as soothing and uneventful as she wished her mind would be. But she couldn't make it be still.

Today it was ambisexual Rory, yesterday it was a postcard that slipped out of the book Charlie was reading. "Sorry you're feeling low. Here's something to cheer you up." On the other side was a reproduction of a Rothko painting, an abstract of solid yellow blocks. Back on the side that really mattered, it was signed, "Janey." She knew who Janey was: a colleague at work. But she didn't know *what* Janey was.

"Nothing. A friend. She left it on my desk."

"After you told her how unhappy you are with me?" Lillian snapped.

"After I'd walked around groaning about my sinuses a couple of weeks ago. Remember? How could I have told her I was unhappy with you? Haven't you noticed that we're happy together?"

"You don't leave cards on someone's desk without a reason."

"Yes, you do. Just a friendly gesture."

"And then you keep it in your book?"

"Yes."

"Why should I believe you?"

"Because I'm telling you the truth."

Charlie's tone of infinite patience frightened her, but there was also something curiously exciting about it. It felt as if she were walking on a smooth lake of ice, knowing that each step brought her nearer to the middle that was not quite frozen enough to be safe. She had wondered on yesterday's walk how many more times they could have that conversation before Charlie threw up his hands and left, his patience turning out not to be infinite at all, as she knew it couldn't be. And now, she recognised suddenly that part of her wished he would. Get it over with. Push him just that bit further, and she wouldn't have to worry about their future; it would be a thing of the past. And she would be proven right: yes, there was love, but it was only up to a point. How could it be any other way?

So this morning it had been Rory. One step nearer. Even if Charlie brought a resplendently masculine Rory round for dinner, there was no reason to believe that he hadn't been seeing someone else, using Rory as an alibi. There was no reason to believe anything, not in a world where outcomes are already inevitable, and telling the truth is the same as telling lies at a different time. Even Charlie's infinite patience was suspect. It was like laying down wine for drinking in the future. The more she grew to trust him, the easier it would be for him to deceive her. It was therefore an act of madness, of self-destruction, to trust Charlie, *even if he was telling the truth.*

The path curved gently around the neat green field and Lillian walked back on the other side towards the entrance. The park had been carved out of the edge of Hampstead Heath. To her left, as she walked, a fence marked the boundary between the untended heath on one side, and the carefully cultivated park on the other. The heath wasn't exactly wild land, there was a network of branching paths through and round it, but Lillian preferred to stay on the cultivated side where there were no unexpected turns along the path, no unforeseen distractions—a circle of interesting mushrooms, or an enticing wooded area—so she could be sure she would be back where she had started from in the same amount of time, every day.

And what was wrong with that? What was wrong with enjoying the thoughtlessness that routine allowed? What was the necessity for doing the unknown, the difficult thing?

Tomorrow, she would overhear Charlie speaking to someone on the phone, while she was having a bath. The next day she'd think she'd detected a scent that wasn't his. The day after, they'd be driving to a restaurant and she'd notice a single, auburn hair on the headrest of the passenger seat. And on. And on. It didn't matter how happy they were together, the suspicions would squeeze out the pleasure, until anxiety was all that was left. Only one thing could satisfy her. Not reassurance, not logic, not re-affirmations of love; only a simple "Yes" in answer to her question would provide relief. Lillian discovered, as she reached the park gate, that was all she wanted. Love was a charming idea, companionship was nice, but only Charlie's infidelity could make her really happy. She was working on it, she thought, as she climbed the stairs to her office. She was doing the best she could to make the relationship work.

## Wide Blue Yonder

It was, Christina thought, the most perfect, the most complete pleasure, physically and mentally (though, currently, it was hard to tell the difference), she had ever experienced. She wondered why she'd never done it before.

It reminded her of how she hadn't got a colour television until she was already the only person she knew who didn't have a video recorder: it wasn't that she didn't want one, but it hadn't seemed to her that she could. Everyone else could, there wasn't a general principle involved. It was that she didn't feel . . . what was it? . . . enough of a grown-up to have a colour television. They—everyone else—seemed properly grown-up to her, but she seemed to herself to be play-acting. They were real and normal, and she was merely apeing them. That was how she felt, and if it crossed her mind to wonder if they were play-acting too, she dismissed it, because they—everyone else—appeared much more comfortable with their roles than she was. So, it didn't feel right for her to be a person with a colour TV.

Now, of course, she had one. It was just a matter of thinking "I can if I want," and buying a set. But it had taken years. Things wouldn't go on like that. The baby wasn't a baby any more; he'd be going to nursery school soon, and once other children were part of his life he'd make sure she knew they could have what everyone else had. Thomas would soon lick her into shape.

But there was the reason she'd waited until her twenty-sixth year before finally trying a float mat. When she was small, they'd been called lilos, and other children's fathers blew them up, cheeks puffing out like Botticelli cherubs, into air-filled plastic ridges. During their occasional days out at the seaside, she'd seen people lying on them, bobbing in the sea, but, even back then, it had never occurred to her that she could lie on one herself. Her parents would have bought her one if she'd thought to ask. At that time, it wasn't exactly about being grown-up, it just didn't seem as if she could do what all the other kids were doing. She'd noticed them, watched them, but her existence seemed so remote from other children's, she hadn't even *wished* she could have a go.

So it had to wait until her middle twenties, and a float mat was propped against the wall, in the porch of their rented cabin in the Caribbean—compliments of the management. It was not the plastic, blow-up, humpy lilo of her youth. This was a high-density foam-rubber bed-length rectangle, turned over on itself and bonded at one end to form a sort of pillow. It was a vivid, cornflower blue, like parts of the sea where it wasn't green or turquoise, like the sky when a passing cloud, or dusk, didn't alter it.

Even so, they were three days into the holiday before she thought of dragging it the ten yards to the beach, very early one morning before Michael and the baby had woken, and flopping it into the water. After that initial effort, it was inevitable—just as entering the electrical department of John Lewis, which she had gone to without any apparent intention, had meant she would inevitably leave with a colour television.

A holiday in the Caribbean was another thing she had supposed, without thinking of it, wasn't for her. Michael had brought it into the realm of possibility. A decent legacy from his aunt meant that, as well as having some savings in the bank, for a rainy day or a bigger house when the next baby came, there was enough to—well, spend.

"Why not?" said Michael, his eyebrows raised semi-circles above the rims of his round spectacles. He waited, giving her his challenging, concertedly boyish look, the one which invited her to participate in his daring and enthusiasm.

Christina couldn't think of an answer except that *other* people went to the Caribbean. But he waved the bank statement at her, and palm trees, clear blue seas, pink sand and coral reefs wafted in front of her own myopia-correcting lenses as a real possibility.

"We could, couldn't we?" she said, as astonished at the truth of what she was saying as she had been when she had presented her credit card to the sales assistant at John Lewis.

So here they were, the three of them, on the smallest island they could discover from a batch of brochures, with their own cabin right on the edge of the beach, and all the picture-postcard views that she'd never really believed existed. Not for her.

Christina was woken early every morning by a tiny black and acid-yellow bird, no bigger than her thumb, which was frantically constructing a nest in a small space between the stone wall of the cabin and an outside light-fitting attached to it just by their sliding glass door. The little creature carried small twigs and bits of fluff from a nearby tree to the light-fitting, and spent ages prodding and poking with its beak, to get each bit meticulously positioned, all the while screeching in a matching acid-yellow voice—Christina supposed in frustration when the twigs and fluff wouldn't stay exactly where it put them. For the first two mornings she got up, put on her bikini, and sat at the table on the porch watching the yellowbird make its nest, leaving her son and husband to sleep on through the racket. On the third morning, however, her gaze wandered to the sky-blue float mat resting against the wall, just below where the yellowbird was working. It didn't seem like a decision when she got up and frightened the yellowbird back into the tree by dragging the float mat across the porch towards the beach.

Getting on it in the water required an act of faith. There was no obvious reason why it wouldn't sink under her weight, or drop at one end or one side, and deposit her in the sea. But it occurred to her, as she stood thigh-deep watching it bob in the shallow surf, that it wouldn't matter: she'd just get wet, and no one was watching. Dignity wasn't an issue. So she flung herself forward and face down onto the mat in the manner of an exhausted, temperamental actress, and it worked—there she was at last, lying on her stomach on the surface of the Caribbean sea.

Christina's small belly and breasts rested in a shallow pool of water which had accompanied her onto the mat—lukewarm, cooling water that took the sharp edge off the sun, which was, even this early, burning down on her shoulders and back. She was still pale. She and Michael had cautioned each other about the dangers of the almost equatorial sun. They kept entirely in the shadows the first day, and spent no more than forty minutes in the sun with their T-shirts on, the second. All three of them wore hats at all times. Now, bobbing at the edge of the sea, Christina remembered she hadn't put any suncream on, but she didn't do anything about it.

She paddled herself out, away from the beach. Not far, just a few feet or so to get a sense she could control the float mat. Checking her position—only a couple of yards from the shore—she felt safe enough to wiggle herself up the mat a little, so that she could put her chin over the edge of the pillowed hump, and look down into the sea. Sunlight rippled through the water to the sand and white rocks at the bottom, and, seeming for a second to be part of the dancing light, a tiny sliver of a fish, electric blue and black, flashed away from beneath her, towards the coral reef a hundred yards beyond. And it was then, at the exact moment when she realised it had been a fish and not a shaft of light, that Christina thought, so sharply, and with such certainty that it took her breath away, that she had never done anything more pleasurable in her entire life. What made this reflection all the more striking was that she knew it was a thought she had never had before.

She skimmed the notable moments in her life. She could think of nothing particular about her childhood. It seemed retrospectively to exist in a silvery-grey haze of good manners; her parents, both academics, nodding and smiling at her as they passed by to disappear into their studies. There were well-tempered outings to see family and colleagues, and holidays in Europe for experience (cities filled with art) or rest (countryside filled with vines). Life was calm and quiet ("Shh, Mummy's working on a paper"), and it was assumed—rightly—that Christina had all the advantages and enough attention to do splendidly at school. Christina and her parents hadn't given each other any surprises. She was the quiet, studious offspring of quiet, studious parents. If she suffered from a slight social awkwardness, that was, they all understood, to be expected in an only child of reasonably superior intelligence.

Getting her degree, then the doctorate: yes, she'd felt pleased, she remembered, although there was hardly any doubt about either. She'd had some sense of achievement, but also a curious darkness had descended—a more intense accretion of darkness with each award, as if she'd been tunnelling, and reached the end only to find another, deeper tunnel beginning immediately.

Michael: she and Michael had been right for each other. They got together almost without noticing it. He, two years ahead of her at university, studying psychology, when she arrived as an undergraduate in the English department. They met through the Film Society, agreeing about Eisenstein and Von Stroheim. A similar taste in books, a mutual disdain for what Michael described with smug contempt as *low culture* (though on her part it was more a lack of information), both serious, inclined to be shy, and poised for academic careers.

Loved Michael? She had not had to choose him from a number of suitors. He was her first, her only boyfriend, and she had made no close friends of either sex at the university. She did not fit in with any of the groups which formed around her. She wasn't disliked, but more overlooked. It was assumed, when anyone thought about it, that she preferred to spend time with her books. Young men didn't find her positively unattractive, but they didn't notice her, or consider her when casting around for female company. There was something a little physically maladroit about the way she moved her thin, angular body through the world, as if her coordination was not quite instinctive but required conscious thought. Her pale face, and even paler, fine hair rose out of clothes which, though tidy and reasonably fashionable, gave the impression of having been purchased by her mother one size too large so that she might grow into them. Once or twice a male student had sat down next to her in the cafeteria, or chatted to her before a film showing, but none did so more than once, or arranged a further meeting.

Except for Michael. He had crossed the cafeteria, ignoring all the empty tables, and put his tray down opposite hers, saying he'd seen her the previous evening at *Potemkin*, and what had she thought of it? For a brief moment, as he sat down and began to speak, Christina viewed him in precisely the way others viewed her. He was thin and not much taller than she, with an unbecoming pallor, though she did notice the eagerness shining in his watery blue eyes in spite of the thickness of his glasses. She had not registered him last night, but remembered having seen him around, in the library and other places, always alone, engrossed in some book or journal, or hurrying on his way to a tutorial. He was not particularly prepossessing, but she couldn't help but feel his energy and the intensity of his interest in Eisenstein's film.

They got on in a mutually embattled way. He expressed an interest in English poetry as well as theoretical psychology. She was writing an essay on "The Lady of Shalott," and they discussed its suitability for a feminist deconstruction. They began to go about together in their spare time, two solitaries who had found each other's availability useful, and Michael announced his more than intellectual interest in her one evening, as they walked back from a screening of *The Blue Angel*, by stepping in front of her to bring her to a halt and pressing his lips so hard against hers that she was forced to part her teeth and allow his tongue free access to the inside of her mouth. After that, it was assumed by both of them that they were a couple, and before very many fumbles had occurred, Christina had taken herself off to the students' GP and asked to be put on the pill.

The consummation was perfunctory: more rushed and worrying than romantic or passionate. But gradually, as they got the hang of it, and with the aid of a book Michael had bought, they settled down to a regular sexual relationship. Michael was attentive and scrupulous about foreplay, explaining to Christina how important it was to allow time for her arousal, which in women was slower and more generalised than it was for men. Sometimes, he suggested alternative positions, though, neither being especially agile, nothing too exotic was attempted. Christina did not dislike having intercourse, at least at the beginning, but, as far as she knew, she never managed to have an orgasm, no matter how solicitous her lover was. Though he pointed out, for their mutual benefit, the exact site of Christina's clitoris, and massaged it assiduously, having explained the mechanism of women's pleasure, Christina failed to experience what he said she was supposed to. However, after a few weeks she began to make very small, tentative cries once an appropriate length of time had elapsed in their coupling, because Michael seemed to feel so strongly about a woman being fulfilled, and she didn't want to disappoint him. The noises were miniature versions of what she had gathered about orgasmic behaviour from some of the more explicit European films of the *nouvelle vague* (Godard, Antonioni, Fellini) which they'd seen together at the Film Society. They seemed to be convincing enough to make Michael, who had also been a virgin before their affair, feel entitled to get on with his own climax. Before that, they had had interminable sex while he worked away at her, waiting with studied patience and some perplexity for her to come, while Christina, to pass the time, tried privately to guess from the rhythm of his thrusts which nursery rhyme he was staying erect by:

*There was an old man called Michael Finnigan*
*He had whiskers on his chinnigan . . .*
*Higgledy piggledy my fat hen*
*She lays eggs for gentlemen . . .*

Very quickly, it seemed there was no question that they would marry; that they would wait until both had gained their doctorate; and that nothing unexpected would intervene in the meantime to prevent the marriage from taking place.

Nothing did.

And then Thomas was born. *Decided* on: when they both had teaching and research work, and her parents had bought them a flat, it was time to have a child. Thomas. She had been even more ungainly during pregnancy, as well as deathly pale from an iron deficiency, but Michael had been devoted and read up on the subject, rubbing her back when it ached, practising with her the breathing technique she would need for a natural birth—though in the event she had a Caesarean on account of her narrow, far-from-child-bearing pelvis. She loved Thomas; of course she loved him. They were a proper family now.

Christina lifted her gaze from the sea bottom and turned her head to look back at their cabin. She saw, instead, the open, circular structure of the hotel bar on the beach which was now no more than a couple of yards distant. A *frisson* of panic ran through her. She had drifted without having had the slightest sensation of travelling. In just a few minutes of inattention the current had floated her a hundred yards or so along the beach, down from where Michael and Thomas were sleeping, and further out, though not so far or fast, but still a good few extra yards, from the shore. There was no danger, she was near enough to swim back to land if she had to, though she was not much of a swimmer. She had got as far as being awarded her hundred yards' certificate at school, but hadn't bothered after that. Sport had not been high on her family's list of priorities. She supposed she could still swim a hundred yards, but, apart from the long and pointless drug-free labour Michael had insisted they try for before giving up and acknowledging the need for the Caesarean section the doctor was urging, she had no evidence that she possessed physical stamina enough for more than that.

Using one hand as a paddle, she turned the float mat to face the shore, and then pushed the water back behind her with both hands to get closer in. She worked her way parallel to the beach, against the current, which was not strong, until she was once again in front of their cabin. As she rolled off the mat and into the shallow water she told herself that, if she did it again, she must remember to keep an eye on where she was. Christina grabbed the mat before it began to float off, and dragged it back over the sand to the porch. The yellowbird was piping for all its worth, but fluttered off as Christina propped the dripping float mat against the wall of the cabin and went inside to take a shower.

That morning, Michael also found a use for the float mat, though if he noticed how sandy it was (the sun dried it off in minutes), he didn't mention it. They were returning from a fraught breakfast, where Michael had taken the opportunity to introduce Thomas to the delights of tropical fruit. ("No, no, no! No cornflakes for you this morning. We're in the land of mangoes and papayas. Yes, you *will* like them. There's nothing to cry about. Mummy, tell him to stop crying! *Try* some, Thomas. Come on, it's part of the adventure.") Thomas was still sniffing back tears at being denied his cornflakes, when to distract him Michael dramatically stopped dead at the entrance to their porch, and pointed at the float mat.

"*What* is that? Eh, Thomas, do you know what it's for?" he said in a rhapsodic voice intended to invoke curiosity and wild surmise in the little boy. Thomas' expression remained neutral as he stared at the float mat. "Come on," Michael said, taking his son by one hand and the mat in the other.

Christina just watched as they walked off, but called out as they got to the sea edge, "Be careful, Michael. Keep hold of him in the water."

Her husband turned with raised eyebrows at her needless warning. His face was the one that told her she was being overprotective and would do her son more harm than good with such an attitude. She sat down at the table and watched her family, one hand shading her eyes, from the porch.

Michael bent down and lifted Thomas, carrying him into the surf as he pulled the float mat behind him with his free hand. Thomas hadn't been to the sea since he was an infant and Christina saw his tiny hands lock in panic around his father's neck as they waded in.

"It's quite safe," Michael said. "I'm holding you. Look, the water's only up to Daddy's knees."

Thomas relaxed and began to enjoy himself from the safety of his father's embrace. He laughed gleefully as a bigger wave than the rest splashed his calves.

"Wet. Wet. Wet," he chortled, scissoring his legs in excitement.

"You see?" Michael grinned at him, speaking in the high, singsong whine he invariably used to the child. "It's lovely, isn't it? This is the sea." He turned to give a brief, satisfied nod to Christina, who allowed her tensed muscles to relax.

"Now then . . . don't worry. Daddy's here, you're safe as houses."

Michael lifted Thomas away from his chest and carefully

put him sitting in the centre of the float mat. Thomas' smile disappeared and a look of terror appeared on his face, but Michael immediately held onto the mat.

"It's all right. See? I'm holding onto you. There's nothing to be afraid off, you can't float away. I'm holding on."

Thomas watched his father's hands on the edge of the mat for a moment, and then, looking cautiously around him, began to enjoy the odd, though faintly familiar feeling of the sea's gentle undulations beneath him. He smiled with pleasure at his new position, as a sense of lording it over the massive and mysterious sea came to him.

"That's it," Michael encouraged. "Look at you. Are you the captain of your ship? Yes, you are!"

Thomas laughed with a gathering hilarity, while the pitch of Michael's affirmations climbed higher and higher, almost to a scream: "Yes, you *are*! Yes, you *are*! *Yes*, you are!"

With each "Yes" Michael extended his arms so that the float mat moved away a little, but he held onto the edge and brought it back in close to his body each time. But on the final "*Yes*," as he straightened his elbows, he let go of the mat after a final shove and it floated free, away from the shore.

For a few seconds Thomas was too caught up in the thrill of the game to take in what had happened. He could see no reason why the squealing and teasing should not go on increasing indefinitely—he was too young to sense that such a crescendo of enthusiasm had to lead to a climax, and, of course, he trusted his father, who had promised to hold tightly onto the mat, who had promised he was as safe as houses. So it was a moment before Thomas realised he was disconnected from his father and alone at the mercy of the sea. Even then it took another instant before the momentum of his childish screams of joy could be halted. The remnants of laughter died in Thomas' throat as he felt the deep power of the sea moving underneath him and realised that there was no steadying, adult hand keeping him in touch with his life. His father had let him go.

Every muscle in Thomas' small body went rigid, and his face transformed into a gaping mask of terror; the open mouth a black, stunned O, the large blue eyes bulging in disbelief. He saw his father, standing still, knee-deep in the water, grinning across the widening distance between them. Michael raised his arm and flapped a limp wrist up and down in mock farewell to his son.

"Bye-bye. Bye-bye, Thomas."

Thomas found his voice, and his mouth, which had locked open after the laughter had so suddenly died, opened wider now to cry out in fear and panic. He screamed so loudly that on the other side of the tiny island people stopped and listened for a moment, wondering if they should go and see what was happening. Christina had been watching the yellowbird and trying to phase out the noise of the hysterical game her husband and son were playing. As Thomas' screams hit her ears, she turned her head sharply and jumped up, ready to run to the rescue. The yellowbird retreated into the neighbouring tree.

Of course, the float mat had not drifted far, barely a few feet, and Thomas was in easy reach of Michael, who was a strong swimmer. It only seemed to Thomas that he had been cast adrift, things looking different, vaster and more distant, from a toddler's perspective on the unfamiliar and insecure surface of the sea. Christina saw at once that there was no actual danger, and even as she looked, Michael had stopped the game and was wading deeper and reaching out for Thomas on the float mat. No more than a minute had passed. Christina watched as Michael scooped the stiff-limbed, howling child into his arms, and splashed with him back to the shore, clucking and laughing scornfully at his son's ridiculous fear.

For the remainder of the holiday by the sea, Christina knew, as her heart returned to its regular rhythm, they would have trouble persuading Thomas to go anywhere near the water. She knew that much of the restfulness of such a holiday was lost now, and that Michael would make a project of reintroducing Thomas to the sea, while she would murmur uneasily that it didn't matter, why not leave it till next year. A stab of anger went through her. *Why* had Michael been so stupid? How could someone who prided himself on his intelligence and who spent his days conducting research into human behaviour have done something so asinine? The answer came as a dull replacement to the sharp edge of anger: because he was an ass. Her husband and Thomas' father was an ass: a fool who thought it funny to frighten a small child, who could not resist the small, mean act of betrayal that proved him more powerful than his four-year-old son.

And that ass was her companion in life; her—the dullness washed through her—*partner.* In a kind of enraged anguish she thought: Why hadn't there been someone else? Why was he the only man who had presented himself to her? The truth was *anyone else* would have been better than Michael, and she'd known that even at the time. But the rage subsided and the dullness returned; no one else had wanted her. The unfairness of it, of who she was, of what life had entitled her to claim for herself, brought painful tears to her eyes which she had to blink back as her husband brought their unhappy son towards her.

Thomas ran to Christina as soon as he was released from Michael's embrace. He wrapped himself around her pale legs and held tight, burying his wet, swollen face, hiding from the impatience of his father. Christina stood frozen, the weight of her son around her calves like an anchor, the weight of the future, as she looked at her husband, even greater.

"He's such a silly baby," Michael said, singsong, sneering, like a playground bully, mocking the childish fears of his victim and inviting his wife into a collusive alliance against their son. "He thought I'd let him float away. I wouldn't let that happen to my baby boy, would I, Mummy? Silly billy, baby . . ."

When the look in Christina's eyes did not change Michael shrugged. The silence in which his words were received made their echo ring, so that his own piping intonation returned to discomfort him. He felt uneasy, caught out, and perhaps became resentfully half-aware of his own meanness of spirit, the smallness and the shame of needing to make a child miserable and frightened so that he might feel superior and adult. So he shrugged at his impassive wife and snivelling child, and marched past them briskly into the cabin to take a shower and peevishly to nurse his annoyance at having been betrayed by Christina, who was supposed to be on *his* side.

An hour later Michael emerged from the cabin. Thomas had calmed down by then, and he and Christina were playing Snap on the porch table. Christina was losing absentmindedly, doing little more than turn her cards over until yelps of triumph from her son told her she had failed to notice a matching card once again. Her lack of involvement in the game didn't matter to Thomas, who was exulting in an orgy of winning.

"I've won again," he squealed, jumping up and down in his seat and gathering the pile of cards towards him. "I've won. I've won. I've won."

Christina managed a distant smile and congratulated him politely.

Michael had that scrubbed look; his hair wetly slicked back, the skin which emerged from his short-sleeved shirt and long shorts, pink and pale against their vivid red and blue. He carried a baseball cap in his hand and swung it on to his head as he stepped into the sunlight. In his other hand was a yellow frisbee. His mood was painfully buoyant.

"All right, team. Let's play frisbee!"

Thomas stopped dealing cards and stared indignantly at his father.

"We're playing Snap."

"What we need around here is a bit of energy." He sounded like a holiday-camp host. "Come on, Mummy. *Come on.* Let's *play.*"

Thomas threw the pack of cards at the table in a temper.

"I want to play Snap," he whined.

"You know what we do when little boys have silly tantrums and won't join in the fun, don't you?" Michael said, taking Christina's wrist and pulling her up. "We ignore them, don't we, Mummy? And we get on with enjoying ourselves without them."

Thomas remained at the table and sulked while Christina and Michael played frisbee. Christina stood just inside the porch and unenthusiastically caught the yellow disc Michael threw at her from the pathway, just by the edge of the beach. Though she retained the same distant smile she'd worn while playing Snap, her insides churned sourly at the sight of Michael's frenetically self-conscious dance: ducking and feinting, jumping from side to side, his arms raised wide, and whooping "Okay! Okay! Come on, you won't get past me!" as he waited to receive the frisbee. He looks demented, she thought, pitching it straight towards him. Michael made a balletic sideways leap into the air and missed the catch.

"Brilliant!" he yelled, awarding his wife praise for so cunning a strategy. "Now, let's see what you can do with this."

He pranced about for several minutes, jerking his arms in pretend throws, and shouting to Thomas to watch how he was going to fool Mummy completely. Thomas didn't look up, but continued to sit with his head on his arms at the table. Christina waited, bored, embarrassed, for the throw. As he finally released the frisbee, and she reached up a listless arm to retrieve it, she wondered if Michael would change over the next twenty years.

Michael had put some kind of spin on the frisbee, so that halfway between the pitch and the catcher, it changed direction, veered to the right of Christina, and landed with a thud on Thomas' lowered, unsuspecting head. He wasn't badly hurt, just slightly grazed over one eye and shocked, but as Christina rushed over to him, the screaming began again.

When she'd got Thomas calm she looked up and saw that Michael was sitting, his legs extended, on a sunbed, in the shade of a palm tree at the edge of the beach, reading some academic papers. He'd undone the buttons on his shirt, which hung loose on either side of his hairless, pink chest, but still wore his baseball cap, navy socks and matching deck shoes. She hated herself for being someone who was married to such a man.

Michael sulked for the rest of the day, which meant, at least, that there were no further dramas, only an atmosphere at dinner when the three of them ate together in an awkward silence at the restaurant under the stars. Later, Christina lay awake next to Michael for several hours, unable to get the thought of the next twenty years out of her mind. She was stuck with the idea that Michael was what she deserved, that they were a true match, and therefore there could be no thought of leaving him.

Two inadequate people had found each other, and the only difference between them was that Christina understood that that was what they were. What it was that made other people adult, adjusted, interesting, was beyond Christina's understanding, and had always been. She'd never felt herself to be okay but could never isolate what it was that was actually wrong with her. She saw herself in the mirror of Michael, and she knew that she was bound to him in matching isolation and gaucheness; doomed, she felt now, to gaze on her reflection through Michael until she took her last breath.

Unconcerned by her lack of sleep, the yellowbird summoned Christina as usual, early the next morning. She only glanced at the nest in passing—for all its hard work, the creature still had a long way to go. Christina didn't sit at the table, but took the float mat and went straight down to the water's edge. The idea of floating on the sea before Michael and Thomas woke was pleasing enough to take the edge off last night's despair. She dropped the mat onto the surface of the water and waded in after it, but then heard someone whistling and footsteps on the gravel path behind her. She knew it wasn't Michael: the whistle was a tuneful, lazy rendition of "Summertime," not for show, but just a relaxed private expression of contentment by someone unselfconsciously at ease with himself. It couldn't be Michael. It would never be Michael.

Christina turned and squinted up the beach. A man in his thirties was walking along the path with a tray in his hands. As he came towards the spot below which Christina stood, ankle deep in the sea, she watched his slow, sun-drenched, bare-footed gait, the small curve of wellbeing on his lips, the openness of his bare, tanned torso to the delicious rays of the sun. It was not that there was anything spectacular about him—he was no better built than average, and not exceptionally handsome.

What struck Christina as she stood and watched him, was how at ease he seemed with himself and how *solidly* he existed. She noticed, as he came to the part of the path by Christina's cabin, the coffee pot and two cups and saucers on the tray. A flash of pain streaked across Christina's forehead as she imagined the sleeping woman who would come awake with fresh coffee seeping into her consciousness. A smile from him as he set down the tray and sat on the edge of the bed, pouring coffee for the two of them. A "Good morning" between them that picked up the warmth of falling asleep in each other's arms last night. They wouldn't have to kiss, not immediately, only to sip coffee and feel drenched in their pleasure at waking up to another day of being together. Christina saw all this in a second of pain, anguished by the knowledge that the woman who would be woken in a few moments was not her.

The man saw her then, stopped whistling, and smiled amiably at her.

"Lovely morning," he called. "Enjoy your float."

Christina managed a smile, but already he had passed by and forgotten her existence. The melody of "Summertime" drifted through the air again and in a moment he had disappeared into his cabin a few doors down from her own.

Christina lay face down on the blue float mat, her arms folded under her chin. If she opened her eyes, she could look down into the water, but for a while she kept them closed so that there was only the sensation of the warm sun along her body and the movement of the waves undulating beneath her, rolling under her body from head to toe, rocking her in a gentle, regular rhythm.

She opened her eyes and stared along the surface of the water. Her head was facing away from the shore, her eyes virtually level with the sea which spread out in front of her, a dense carpet of aquamarine as far as she could see. She floated, nothing more than a pair of eyes, in the centre of this uninterrupted vista, watching small waves make hummocks that rolled towards her lazily, over and over, the sea repeating itself tirelessly, endlessly. She dropped her arms and let them float in the water at either side of her and looked down. The sea was perfectly clear and landscaped beneath the surface in breathtaking colour. She took a deep breath and dipped her face into the water, keeping her eyes open. The coral waved amoebic arms and delicate fernlike fronds at her, their pinks, greens and yellows so outrageously vivid that they might have been painted; neon-bright fish, mostly tiny, fleeting shapes like streaks of lightning, but some surprisingly large and languorous, wove in and out of the swaying forest of coral.

Christina lifted her head and, smiling utter contentment to herself, let her eyes close again. She allowed the sea and warmth to drift her into daydream. The man with the tray of coffee was beside her, bobbing on the water next to her. He let his arms fall into the water and their hands met below the surface. They belonged to each other, easily and safely. She thought of the next twenty years and more of being together and it was as if the sun had seeped through her skin and was shining inside her.

Christina began to feel her shoulders burning and carefully rolled herself over on the mat to lie on her back. The mat bounced for a moment and then settled back into its regular, gentle movement. Enough water had slopped onto it to relieve and cool her overheated skin. She had to shade her eyes with her hand against the brightness of the sun before opening them. The blinding disc of light and heat blazed down at her from an unbroken blue sky, as continuous and horizonless as the sea had been when she had lain face down. The sun was almost directly above her now, she noticed, turning her head to one side to rest her eyes. The sea and sky met far off into the distance. She turned her head to look in the other direction and saw the same panorama stretching away. After a moment, she lifted her head a little and looked along the length of her body. Again, there was only sea and sky. She did not have to turn around to know that the same view would meet her eyes if she looked behind her. She lay back and splashed some water onto her belly, watching through the screen of her lashes as the last iridescent drops of water fell from her dangling fingers. When she felt pleasantly cool again, she closed her eyes and relaxed, leaving her arms to drag weightily in the sea. This was, she thought, the most complete pleasure she had ever experienced. She wondered why she'd never done it before.

# On the Existence of Mount Rushmore and Other Improbabilities

The thought came to Ellen in the middle of one night. First she was asleep and then she was awake with a single question in her head, as if it was asking itself so urgently it couldn't wait until morning to have itself thought about. The question was this: Does Mount Rushmore exist? And then, in answer to her weary: Well, of course it exists, a supplementary question: How do you know?

Got her! That was the end of the night's sleep. It didn't matter how much she told herself that she couldn't care less about Mount Rushmore, had never given Mount Rushmore more than a passing thought, and firmly turned on her side to get back to sleep, it just wouldn't go away. She sat up, lit a cigarette and the bedside lamp, and gave it a passing thought.

All she could think about Mount Rushmore was that Cary Grant and whatwashername—Eva Marie Saint—had crawled all over it trying to get away from . . . James Mason, she thought, in *North By Northwest*. They had clambered across the faces of American presidents carved into the mountainside in—she didn't know where. Which presidents? Lincoln, she was sure, but who else? She didn't remember, if she'd ever known. Why should she? She lived and worked in London, England. She didn't have to know about Mount Rushmore. Except that she'd been woken up, and her night's sleep ruined worrying about it.

She wished Martin hadn't taken his *Encyclopaedia Britannica* with him when they split up. She missed that more than she missed him. Tomorrow she promised herself, she would go to the library at school and check it out. *Now*, could she please go to sleep?

The trouble is, once you've turned on the light and smoked a cigarette, you have to watch the dawn come in through the venetian blinds. It was a law of some kind. She stared grimly at the blackness seeping through the cracks in the slats.

Until last year, she had been a history teacher. She worked, still worked, though now in the English department, at a comprehensive school of the kind the local middle-class parents managed not to send their children to. Since everyone had to stay at school until sixteen, and it was not permissible to tell children they didn't have a hope of getting decent grades at GCSE and they'd be better off going out and earning a living, she had been in charge of a bunch of sixteen-year-olds who were supposed to be studying for the exam. None of them was very bright, but Tracy was the least able of them all. Her dimly-lit face never seemed illuminated with thought, but she was pleasant and worked heartbreakingly hard. It always surprised Ellen how much effort Tracy put into her work, in spite of never achieving anything more than a pat on the back for trying.

Everybody had to do a project for history, which counted

for twenty per cent of the final exam. Tracy was doing the project Ellen always suggested to the least academic kids: Costume in the Eighteenth Century. They liked going to the library, and, with the help of the librarian, finding books with plenty of pictures. For over six months Tracy had been copying dresses, shoes, hats, coats and underwear from books and colouring them in, her tongue poked concentratedly between her lips. The folder was quite thick now. There were dozens of drawings, each labelled as neatly as she could manage in her tentative, round handwriting. Every time Ellen passed her desk, she would stop and make admiring noises about Tracy's use of colour, which was all she could find to make an honestly positive comment about.

Then, one day, Tracy had lifted her head from her work while Ellen was across the other side of the room.

"Miss," she called out. This was the usual long drawn out "Mi . . . isss" which signified a problem. Ellen went to Tracy's desk.

"Mi . . iss," Tracy repeated when Ellen bent down to look at the work. "You know the eighteenth century . . . ?"

This was the usual form of words for all the pupils. All queries or statements began with "You know . . ." and then the subject of the forthcoming discussion. Ellen had long since stopped making a point about this, and these days, answered, "Miss, you know my mum . . . ?" or even, on occasion, "Miss, you know God . . . ?" in the affirmative. It was the only way to get on with it. They would not continue until she had said yes, so she said yes.

"Yes," Ellen said, with a little more truth than usual. She was a history teacher, and she did know something about the eighteenth century. "What about the eighteenth century, Tracy?"

"Well, was it before or after the war, Miss?"

Ellen stayed very still while she took in Tracy's question. For a moment she was going to ask, "Which war?" but decided against it. She knew, in the kind of rush in which revelation arrives, that for Tracy there would be only two wars: the first and the second. And since there was nothing before one, those would be the only two she knew about. Or rather, not about, but knew of their existence. Tracy continued to look up at her teacher, waiting expectantly for an answer.

A thought struck Ellen.

"Why do you want to know?"

Why *did* she want to know? If she didn't know when the eighteenth century was, what difference did it make which war it was before or after?

"I dunno," Tracy said, sorry now that she'd asked and been obliged therefore to answer a question herself. "I just wondered."

Late that night, Ellen sat at her kitchen table and forced herself to be inside the mind of Tracy. It seemed very important to get an inkling of what it might be like to have no concept of chronology beyond one's own birthdays. That it had never crossed *her* mind that Tracy (and others, certainly) did not know where the eighteenth century was in relation to the present day, seemed to Ellen a level of ignorance close to Tracy's. So she set about trying to imagine how the world was for her pupil.

She was surprised to find that inside Tracy's mind, it was not, as she'd imagined, all empty space and fog. On the contrary, it was extraordinarily crammed in there. There were countless tiny doors inside Tracy's mind, so many it would be impossible to investigate them all in a single session. But it wouldn't have been feasible anyway, because each of the doors Ellen tried was locked, and there were no corridors leading from one to another. She began to get a picture of how it worked.

Tracy, like all the kids, watched countless hours of television, preferably American imports, but sometimes she would see something set in a different historical period. At first, Ellen wondered how she would understand the nature of the drama she was watching. But then she realised that what happened was that Tracy watched the historical drama from one of the rooms in her mind, and when, say, *Baywatch* was on, she viewed it from a different room. She could only be in one room at a time, and had no access to what was behind the other doors. So she would watch an episode of *Sherlock Holmes*, more or less following the story, but without any context, because each piece of information on the Victorian period which had made its way into her mind during the course of her life lived separate and alone in one of the rooms behind a locked door. There was nothing but pure narrative, or disembodied detail in Tracy's worldview.

Presumably, some circuit had shorted, and briefly connected one room with another, which had caused her to ask about the relationship between the eighteenth century and the war. And this was why she had been so confused when Ellen asked her why she wanted to know. Tracy had no idea why she wanted to know. It was just that a door had swung open, and a question popped out.

Tracy would not get her GCSE history. But she would get a job, marry, have children and take care of a home; and she'd do most, if not all, of those things as well as Ellen would. Tracy would be perfectly able to enjoy and manage her life. It was only that she wasn't suited to learning things she had no need to know about.

That was when Ellen changed from the History to the English department. In the English department then there was no syllabus to be got through. The year she had spent explaining about the Industrial Revolution would be replaced by the entertainment of reading stories (knowing them to be contextless for many, but stories nevertheless) and doing practical exercises which young people who are about to manage life on their own would find useful. Writing applications for job interviews; filling in forms; keeping diaries . . .

When Ellen had told the story of Tracy to Martin—who was still living with her at the time—he told her the story about one of *his* history classes; a group of fourteen-year-old boys. He'd been about to start teaching the voyages of discovery, and was setting the pre-Columbian scene, explaining to them how people believed that the world was flat. He'd noticed a funny look in several of the boys' eyes, and something cold had run down his spine, he said. So he pointed round the room and asked each boy whether the world was flat or round.

The first boy looked panic-stricken.

"Round, Sir . . . No, flat, Sir . . . Um . . ."

Thirteen of the twenty-seven boys were uncertain.

"*Uncertain,*" Martin emphasised. "None of them positively believed the world was flat, but only because they didn't believe anything at all about the planet. They simply never thought about it. And, you know what? They're right. It doesn't matter one way or the other to them. Or to us. Everything works just fine. They and we get on with our lives. They climb aboard aeroplanes and fly to sunny parts of Europe, even to America, some of them. But they don't think about falling off the edge because planes fly from airport to airport. The shape of the earth is irrelevant. It could be hexagonal, for all they care, as long as they get where they want to go."

And when she came to think about it, knowing that the earth was spherical and that the eighteenth century came before the nineteenth century wasn't information she actually used much in her life. She could have got on perfectly well without it. She tried to remember the moment when she had been taught those facts, but she couldn't because there wasn't a moment. It was as if she'd always known them. And so what? Had the world really turned upside down when Columbus didn't fall off the edge of the earth, or did most people simply shrug when they heard the news? *And so what?* In fact, most people wouldn't have heard about it. They would have lived through the discovery, got on with their business, and died without ever knowing the cataclysmic news.

Ellen saw the first dim glow of light coming through the gaps in the venetian blinds. *Mount Rushmore*, she thought again. What an extraordinary thing to do to a mountain. And how, in God's name, had they done it? How could a team of stonemasons, or sculptors, or explosives experts, or whatever they were, have made the mountainside Abraham Lincoln look anything like Lincoln on such a scale? And why? To celebrate America and democracy, she supposed. Or some such idealistic motive. Probably not unlike the idealistic motives she'd had in the seventies that made her go into teaching.

Now she came to think of it, Mount Rushmore was the silliest thing she could imagine. Odd, really, that she'd never thought of it before. Not in all her life, not even during the several times she'd seen *North By Northwest*, had it crossed her mind to wonder about it. For all she knew, it didn't actually exist. After all, Hitchcock would have mocked the thing up in a studio to shoot the final scenes. Its appearance in a film didn't prove its existence. Tomorrow, she'd go (sleepily, for sure) to the library during lunchbreak and find out about it. And what if it didn't really exist? What if Mount Rushmore was nothing more than a Hollywood set: just an idea? What if I dreamed it up, she thought with sleep grasping at her mind; what then?

# Sex and Drugs and Rock 'n' Roll: Part II

Time, Constance decided, was not cyclical, but more like a spiral. It was not so much that time repeated itself, round and round, and over and over again, but that it *almost* did. Which suggested to her that there probably was a God, or at any rate an omnipotent Critic.

The nature of the spiral is that it very nearly comes full circle, but stops short of the absolute circumference, and creates another near circle that doesn't make it. It was the gap between the end of one almost-circle and the next which convinced her that she was inhabiting a more than physical universe. At the place where the circles didn't meet up, where the cycle refused to complete itself, was the commentary: the chiming laughter that could be harsh or indulgent, but, in either case, rang in her ears like the toll of a ghostly clock.

The trouble was that there was more than one cycle and

their numbers grew as she got older, so that it seemed to her that, these days, there was hardly a gap between the periods of laughter bouncing off the walls. No time to rest from noticing. Sometimes she thought she would have liked to inhabit a linear planet where what was done was done for good or bad and then it was on to the next thing. But it seemed that by the time life was officially halfway through it was so clogged with near repetition there was hardly any possibility of just getting on with whatever was next. Lately, she had come to suspect that *nothing* was next; only a rolling retrospective. Life wound up, and then it wound down.

In some frames of mind, this notion was not unpleasing to her. It allowed her to sit and watch, and, the truth was, she really didn't like things happening, not things she wasn't expecting. She hoped for a middle and old age without surprises.

Nonetheless, she was sitting at the kitchen table with three cigarette papers, trying to remember how they were supposed to fit together.

"Let me have a go."

This was a reasonable request as Rosie was much better at spatial stuff. One of the benefits of having brought her into the world was that Constance no longer had to wrap Christmas presents. Rosie always did it for her and was much more economical and neat about it.

Constance had never rolled a joint in her life. She had always got someone else to do it because she was incapable of making one that even remotely resembled something that could be smoked. She didn't think it was a necessary skill to have since, in 1968, there had been plenty of talented joint rollers around, and in the last twenty years, though she kept a little hash about, she never found herself needing a smoke so urgently that if there wasn't anyone around she suffered for the lack of it. The hash on the table was eighteen months old. She wondered if it had gone off.

But now, in these circumstances, she felt the need for rolling skills because she thought she ought to be in charge of the process. However, working out the ought of these circumstances was precisely her problem, for the only ought that she could be sure of was that these circumstances ought not to have arisen. And yet they had, with an inexorability that confirmed her theory of spiral time. The laughter had already started.

She pushed the papers across the table to her thirteen-year-old daughter and busied herself with tearing off the underside of the lid of the cigarette packet, rolling it into a compact cylinder to make a tip.

"What a talent we have for organisation," she said, knowing that the only way to forestall the laughter was to nail down the absurdity out loud. "We should go into business together."

Rosie was too busy concentrating on the cigarette-paper puzzle to answer. Anyway, for her it was a serious business.

"Why can't you use just one paper?" she muttered, although she had just got the hang of it.

A good question. In the days when she was doing this stuff she hadn't thought to wonder.

"It's traditional," Constance said, cutting off another protoplasmic chuckle from on high.

This arm of the spiral began when Rosie came home from school and asked, "What's a spliff?"

Answering people's questions as nearly truthfully as possible had become a habit with Constance. It wasn't a question of morality; more that it was easier and less confusing in the long run. On these grounds Constance had always answered Rosie's questions truthfully whenever possible. The first signs that this might bring a difficulty all of its own had occurred the previous year while Rosie was leafing through a woman's magazine. She looked up.

"It tells you how to do blow jobs," she said, astonished, her upper lip contracting with distaste.

Constance blinked at her twelve-year-old. "What do you know about blow jobs?"

Rosie was dismissive. "Everyone knows what blow jobs are." Very sophisticated. "It's *disgusting.*" Not so sophisticated. And a question, "*Isn't* it disgusting?"

Constance felt like dirty bathwater swirling down a plughole. She could see what was coming, but what was to be done about it? She switched to the evasion principle of child-rearing.

"Well," she said with a shrug that did nothing to relieve the sudden tension in her neck, "it's a normal part of sexual activity."

"It's *disgusting,*" Rosie insisted. "You wouldn't do that, would you?"

Now Constance was in the very centre of the whirlpool.

"It's a normal part of sexual activity," she repeated without hope.

Rosie stared at her mother in disbelief. Constance felt trapped for both of them. She was certain that children didn't want to know about their mother's sex lives. Why had Rosie asked? A wave of anger went through her, aimed at Rosie, who she felt should have known better. Telling the truth depended on the good sense of people not to ask the questions they didn't want to know the answers to.

Rosie began to cry and raced upstairs to her bedroom. She wouldn't let Constance kiss her goodnight. The next day she came home from school eating a Mars Bar. Constance welcomed her at the door and bent down for a bite. Rosie snapped the Mars Bar from Constance's reach.

"Get your own. I know where your mouth's been."

They'd got over it. It hadn't been mentioned again, but Constance had heard hoots of laughter squeezing into the space that was left between Rosie's Mars Bar and herself at twelve, trying, but being unable, to imagine her parents, *her parents*, doing it. Very funny.

So when Rosie asked, "What's a spliff?" Constance was prepared for the spinning in her head to start.

"You mean dope?"

"I don't know. You smoke it or make brownies out of it."

"You mean dope," Constance sighed. "Who smokes it or makes brownies out of it?"

Rosie's friends did, or some of them said they did and suggested that the others try. There was talk of acid, too. In a panic Constance tried to remember being thirteen. She smoked in the school boilerhouse—Black Russian, because style was of the essence—but no dope. There wasn't any around then. She didn't have her first joint until she was fifteen. After that, for a while, there was no stopping her: no substance that she wouldn't put into her body; no risk she wouldn't take. But that, she remembered, as if she were watching archive film, was because she had been terminally angry at the time and dedicated to the task of self-destruction.

Rosie wasn't angry. Her interest in dope was the equivalent of Constance's cigarettes in the boilerhouse—a matter of style. She played Constance's gouged recordings of the Velvet Underground and Jefferson Airplane; she carried her books to school in a sack made of a remnant of mirrored, silver-threaded cloth of eastern origin; she burned incense in her room while she did her homework. But Rosie wasn't raging against the world or looking as far afield as possible for some kind of life that made more sense than the one she'd been allocated. And Rosie didn't want to die.

All the things that Rosie wasn't should have made Constance proud of the job she'd done. That her daughter wasn't a twitching, melancholy, suicidal mess was an indication that Constance had done better than her own mother. But, as Constance pointed out to anyone who said so, to be proud of that was like coming home flushed with the day's success because one hadn't been run down by a lorry. Rosie made Constance uneasy, precisely because she was amiable, positive and lacked the desire to tear her world (and herself) to pieces. Constance waited, moment by moment, as if holding her breath, for the trouble to begin. The "What's a spliff?" question was the starting pistol. Now, it would begin. Constance steadied herself with the thought that she had survived. Probably, Rosie would, too. Probably.

And yet it wasn't the beginning of anything that Constance recognised. Rosie wanted information. She took in Constance's warning about acid and hard drugs and alcohol, nodding impatiently.

"Well, *of course* I wouldn't use that stuff, I don't want to ruin my life. I was just thinking of having a spliff once a fortnight or so. At weekends," she added.

Constance stared at her daughter, not knowing what to say next to this orderly adolescent. Liberalism and logic came to the rescue in spite of Constance's inner knowledge that there was something very wrong with the conversation.

"Well, in that case, you ought to know how to use the stuff."

It made sense. Rosie was going to try it anyway. She'd better know how much to use and what to do with it.

So the lesson commenced. In the bright light of the kitchen, tobacco was released from a cigarette and spread on the paper; the dark lump of hash was burned enough to make it crumble and Rosie watched carefully as not very much was added to the tobacco. It was not unlike the time that Constance had shown her how to separate egg yolk from the white. Rosie's dexterous fingers rolled the paper around the mixture, pushed the tip into one end and twisted the other. There it was.

"But I've never smoked," Rosie suddenly remembered.

Constance spread her arms wide and lifted her shoulders in a fatalistic gesture.

"It won't get me addicted to cigarettes, will it?"

"Not once a fortnight at weekends, I shouldn't think."

Constance lit the twisted end and inhaled a couple of times. Then she handed the joint to Rosie, who took it gingerly, holding the smoking cylinder at arm's length as if it might explode. The look on her face suggested she was about to take some particularly nasty medicine. She craned her neck forward rather than bringing her hand to her mouth as if that would keep the smouldering joint at a safe distance, and took the tiniest puff. Immediately, she started coughing and flung the joint away from her on to the table.

"It's horrible!" she yelled and dashed out of the room. A few moments later she came back, having brushed her teeth to get rid of the foul smell of tobacco on her breath. But she was ready to try again, determined to get on with the learning process. Altogether, she brushed her teeth three times before the joint was finished, and inhaled almost nothing. With every inhalation, each more tentative than the last, she choked and pushed the joint towards Constance to get it out of her hands. By the third puff Constance had started laughing at their kitchen comedy; by the fourth Rosie joined in, between bouts of coughing.

Constance didn't feel much effect. It looked as if the dope had had its day.

And wickedness seemed to have had its day, too. Comedy had taken over and Constance and Rosie's laughter combined with another peal that didn't come from either of them. This was how it was, then, Constance supposed, looking across at Rosie who, still giggling, had given up trying to smoke the joint and was waving it in the air, making pretty curling patterns with the smoke. Constance could see her own features in her daughter's smiling, rueful, slightly flushed face. She watched Rosie's eyes follow the column of smoke she had made rise and twirl in the air; they were the same eyes that stared back at Constance when she looked in the mirror. Constance followed the smoke with her own eyes until, at the top, it lost formation and wafted away to invisibility. What did the twisting coil remind her of?

She looked back at Rosie and saw the tiny baby she had been. And before that, inside her, the foetus that had grown from an undifferentiated cell. And before *that*, her own chromosomes, dividing; a reduction in preparation for reproduction. But, down there in the land of chemical bases, the intertwining double helix had no interest in irony. The similarity and dissimilarity between Constance and Rosie was accidental to DNA's essential task of ensuring its own reproduction. It was a humourless business.

Constance looked around her and saw, not the two of them sitting at either side of the table, but the teeming, whirling millions that really inhabited the kitchen. She was stuck for a moment in the turbulence of a chaotic, microcosmic world: as real as real could be. Then she heard the laughter again, coming from she didn't know where, but sounding close in her ear, like a booming whisper, and she was back in the place of process and repetition; held tight in the spiral of time and comedy, and grateful for both.

Constance wiped the residual tears of her own laughter from her eyes. She took the joint from Rosie's fingers, disrupting the pattern of smoke, and ground it out in the ashtray.

"Well, there it is," Constance said to her daughter, with a smile. "That's drugs. Now, about sex . . ."

# The Old Princess

Long ago the old princess had stopped the clocks in her tower. First, in the early hours of one sleepless dawn, the one in her room at the top of the winding stairs, and then, some years later, when she realised the door was no longer secured (had it ever been?), the big chiming clock down on the lowest landing. What was the point of saving herself from having to hear the seconds tick-tocking away in her room, like raindrops on a window, or tears down a cheek, if every hour, on the hour, the chimes downstairs rang out?

Once both clocks had been stilled, the passage of time was marked only in large, slow movements of the seasons; though she had noticed lately how rapidly even the seasons had taken to coming around. She would look out of her turret window and think, "Is it spring already?" as the greening trees in the forest surrounding the tower told her it was. And then, hardly a few days later, it seemed, she would wonder that winter and its stark, frozen branches had arrived so soon and unexpectedly. When spring came round again, the greenness was renewed, but her heart no longer leapt with ancient relief at the coming alive of the world so reliably once more.

She had been waiting, after all, for a very long time; for as long as she could remember, and possibly longer than that. So long, in fact, that she had almost forgotten what it was she was waiting for.

In many ways, she had been fortunate. Her keepers, whom she never saw, provided food which appeared through a small flap of the great oak door of her tower room at regular intervals, as did clean laundry, washing equipment and towels. She lacked for nothing to keep herself clean and healthy. In addition, every week, for as far back as memory went, a parcel of books appeared through the flap, which she would read and then (after she'd read a book on the history of library catalogues) arrange alphabetically by author or subject, depending on whether they were fiction or nonfiction, on the shelves covering the walls of her room.

Once, on her tenth birthday, a kitten arrived, mewling through the flap with a label round its neck saying: *Happy Eleventh Birthday*. That week, the parcel of books included one about what happens to the bodies of young girls at puberty, so she wasn't altogether surprised when her first period arrived. Neither, it seemed, were her keepers, who from then on provided sanitary towels once a month with the clean laundry. Some pages had been torn out of the book, and what she read failed to explain why the changes were occurring, only that it was completely normal. Later, she understood that princesses in waiting had to remain innocent, even if their bodies were obliged to conform to nonregal standards.

She called the kitten Dinah after a cat in a book she had read. It came and curled up, purring, on her lap and she enjoyed its company. After that, cat food arrived along with her own through the flap. Nothing else came, but she seemed to have everything she needed while she waited. The princess knew she was waiting because she had read in her books, which were a motley but comprehensive selection, about princesses in towers, and knew that waiting was what they did. I'm a princess in waiting, she told herself, stroking Dinah thoughtfully.

For a long time she was perfectly content. But once her sixteenth birthday had passed, a certain restlessness came over her. She had been half expecting something to happen. One morning, she supposed, she would find the door to her room open and during her investigation of the castle she would discover a turret room with an old woman in it, spinning cloth. But her door never opened, and no sharp instrument appeared on which she might prick her finger and thus set the wheels of her destiny in motion. The princess and Dinah grew into young woman– and cat-hood quite undisturbed by the world outside.

When the restlessness came over her, the princess would confide to Dinah with a sigh that she wished something would happen. Dinah would merely purr her contentment back to her mistress. "It's all very well for you," the princess would say tetchily. "You're not a princess." She had never read a story of a cat with a destiny (*Puss in Boots* not having come through the doorflap), but every single story about princesses was, so far as she could see, deeply concerned with the subject of their destiny.

After the eleventh birthday there were no further birthday presents, and eventually the princess lost count of her years, though she noticed changes in herself. Her flesh became rounder, her bones less prominent, as her hips widened and her breasts grew. When she looked at herself in the polished brass plate on the wall, she hardly recognised the little girl she used to see—and in any case, she didn't have to stand on the wooden stool now. Of course, these changes were gradual, and her self-inspection an almost daily habit, so she was not under the impression that someone quite different had come along and taken her, or the other person's, place. It was only when her memory took large jumps into the past that she realised that she had been at least two people while waiting in her tower. And then, later still, there were three. The rounded flesh loosened and lost its tone, her bones became, once again, more prominent, her face narrower and more angular. Her bright blonde hair faded to a colour that was more like the dust hanging on to the cobwebs in the corners and her eyes failed to light up the polished brass with their sparkle as once they had.

It was then that she stopped the clock in her room. She found herself waking in the early hours, her lips tingling with the touch of warm alien flesh, only to discover she was alone as usual and the clock was ticking with an insistent loudness in the silence of the night. Dinah continued to purr, though she was older and scrawnier, too. It came upon her that, in spite of all the books telling her about princesses in towers and other waiting areas, and their eventual discovery, she was a princess to whom nothing was going to happen. There had not been a single story about such a princess, and she was wholly unprepared for such a special destiny. It seemed to her extraordinary—in the sense of outrageous—that she should be the exception to such a universal rule among princesses. Why was it that she was different? Why her?

She came across no answer to this question in any of her books, though she took to re-reading the Psychology and Genetic Sciences sections with some attention. Eventually, she had to admit to herself that it was simply the case that she alone among princesses lacked a destiny; and then she discovered that the door to her turret was not locked. She used the revelation to put a stop to the chiming of the big clock on the lower landing, and then returned to her room, where she found her clean laundry waiting for her, just inside the doorflap. For some time now there had been no sanitary towels.

A new idea came to her. What if there were other princesses in other towers, scattered here and there, who also waited in vain? Perhaps the stories had simply omitted to tell about her sort of princess, or, simply by chance, she had never received those stories through the doorflap. There might be many princesses to whom nothing had ever happened, and who simply lived in their towers day by day. Perhaps their towers were too far off the beaten track for destiny to find them; or it might be that destiny was a limited commodity, and while every princess waited, not all of them could be accommodated. There might be hundreds—thousands—like her. Who could tell, there might even be more of her kind of princess than the sort for whom destiny finally arrived. She began to see that the problem was with the books, and felt some resentment at her keepers for having provided her with stories which took only part of the truth into account. There was no reason, of course, to write about princesses such as her: a life of waiting without an end was not the stuff that stories were made of, but it did give an unbalanced view and a possibly unreasonable expectation to those princesses whose destiny failed to turn up. The provision of books, she felt, was a mistake. She left a note with her soiled laundry to explain this to her keepers.

One morning, the princess woke to find that Dinah had died in the night. The cat lay at the foot of the bed, as if asleep, but she wasn't breathing and took no interest when breakfast came through the doorflap. The princess knew about death: she had read about it. She knew that life had its limit, and that beyond the boundary of old age there was an absence of life. She recognised it immediately in Dinah, whom she stroked for old times' sake. She would miss her only companion—even though it was similar to the ticking of the clock, she had enjoyed Dinah's purring; the sense and sound of another living thing in her life. But Dinah had reached the boundary of her existence and would purr no more.

The princess carried Dinah across the room and put her through the doorflap, and, as she did so, she had a sudden sense of excitement. *Something* had happened to Dinah after all these years. Something *had* happened to her friend, the cat.

The following morning, the princess was woken by a mew. She thought for a moment it was Dinah, and then when she was more fully awake, that she must have been dreaming of her old companion, because she remembered that Dinah was dead. But there was another mew, and when she lifted herself off the pillow, she saw a kitten standing by the doorflap, demanding that someone pay it attention. The princess picked the little creature up and held it in her arms, where it immediately began to purr. So, she thought, Dinah has died, and now there's another cat. What a busy life it was.